FAIRY HEARSED

MISTBROOK MANOR COZY MYSTERIES

A.N. SAGE

Fairy Hearsed

Mistbrook Manor Cozy Mysteries, book 3

Cover and interior art by Cauldron Press

www.cauldronpress.ca

© A.N. Sage and ansage.ca

Contents

Chapter One

The way the sun blazed through the stained-glass windows of the funeral home made my heart pitter-patter with excitement. It was an exceptional view, if you didn't object to the occasional dead body, that is. I pulled the tea towel from the steaming hot teapot and inhaled deeply. The scent of lavender tea wafted through the manor's kitchen, making every nerve in my body awaken. Being a fairy meant that I was intricately connected to all natural things, and that included the lavender I grew on the grounds that I later steeped into my homemade tea blends. Gardening and tea were my two most precious hobbies.

When I wasn't busy running the Mistbrook Manor Funeral Home, of course.

"Your guests are getting feisty," a feline voice drawled from the kitchen doorway.

I spun around to find Theo, my resident changeling slash talking cat lounging in the wide oak frame of the open door. Behind him, more of the afternoon sunlight streamed through the main hallway of the manor, limning his gray fur in a golden hue and making the cat appear almost deity-adjacent. As though Theo needed any more reason to think highly of himself. I was nearly convinced that his stuck-up attitude was the reason he was trapped in a cat's body here on Earth no matter how often he tried to convince me otherwise. Professional disagreement my wings! I had it on good authority that Theo got into a petty argument with a fairy working the changeling assignments and ended up in a cat's body instead of a human child as punishment.

Served him right.

"Hello? Are you buffering?"

I shook my head at the annoying furball. "What do you mean by feisty?" I asked. "What's happened?"

"The ancient one set off the angry one and they've been arguing for a while now."

I cringed. Being an undertaker myself, I assumed all others in the profession had a similar personality to my own—calm and controlled. Unfortunately, I had recently found out how wrong I was to think that. Then again, a secret society of undertakers that solved crimes was not exactly a marker for character. The strange group I fell in with by accident after following the curious case of a dead body from my morgue was nothing if not special. They would have to be to band together and do what they did.

I thought of all the cases we helped solve since I joined the Grim Wardens—a fitting name—and a smile tugged at the corners of my lips.

It was nice to have a deeper purpose in life. And it certainly took my mind off the other trouble knocking at my door. A flash of the portal I accidentally opened with my fairy magic zoomed through my memories. Where did it lead? The icy realm I glimpsed through the portal's doorway held no answers and since the portal shut as quickly as it had opened, I had yet to figure it out.

I shook off the thought and focused my attention on Theo. One problem at a time.

Picking up the tray of tea I had prepared, I locked eyes with the cat and said, "Lead the way. Let's get this sorted before they tear the manor apart."

I padded after the cat, my feet soft on the polished wood floors that creaked under my weight. On either side of me the rose-patterned wallpaper drew my attention and made my brain rattle as I thought about the garden I kept out back. The one where the roses I nurtured changed colors of their own accord for no particular reason. Another problem I'd been putting off dealing with. My magic had been haywire for a while now and I had no clue how to fix it let alone what the underlying issue was. If I was back home in Fairy I could have simply asked my mother for advice, but since I fled the realm in a panic, I had no one but myself to count on.

Orchard Hollow, the town I set my roots in, may have been a hub for paranormal creatures but, as far as I knew, I was the only fairy around.

Actually, that wasn't true anymore.

"I never said that!"

The shrill voice of Ellie Blackwood pierced down the hallway, shaking the antique frames and oil paintings on the walls like an earthquake.

I rolled my eyes. *Here we go again.*

The tray shook as my hands tremored upon entry into the living room. To my left, the towering bookcase was half empty with almost all my personal collection of books spread out over the floor and side tables. There was a Warden near each high pile of tomes, their attention either on the book they perused or picking out their next read. When Mortimer, the oldest member of the group, suggested we start a book club I thought he meant a regular one. But nothing was normal with the undertakers. What Mortimer actually implied was that we spend a day each week at each other's homes acquainting ourselves with the books we all kept. In case a case pops up that might require knowledge we had at our fingertips. His words, not mine.

Don't get me wrong, I enjoyed reading as much as the next sane person, but I was quite busy these days.

My gaze flicked to Finn O'Malley sitting in the wide armchair in the corner. The morgue director's thin shirt strained to envelop his thick arms as he flipped the pages of the poisonous plant encyclopedia I acquired in an antique bookshop in town. His tousled hair hung lower today, nearly past his ears, and he raked his fingers through it when it fell to shadow his stormy eyes. I gulped, heat rising to my cheeks.

I supposed there was a good side to these book club meetings.

"I specifically heard you say precisely that," Mortimer corrected from his token spot on the loveseat alongside the bay window. The undertaker was dressed in his usual less than casual attire, a five-piece suit that looked as if it leaped off the pages of a magazine and tailored itself perfectly to his slender frame. His white-washed hair was gelled to perfection atop his head and barely moved as he shook his head at his opponent. "Or are you calling me a liar?"

"If the shoe fits," Ellie retorted.

The young woman stuck her tongue out at Mortimer. Her thin black glasses slid down her sharp nose and she used her middle finger to push them back up, a gesture I was sure was meant for Mortimer. If the undertaker noticed it, he didn't make a move. Ellie steamed, folding her arms over her chest, the button-down striped shirt she wore wrinkling slightly. She breathed out a frustrated sigh and snapped the black suspenders holding up her pleated wide pants. "You are impossible."

"Me?" Mortimer asked, his hands up in surrender. His eyes flashed to me. "Oh, good. Lyra is back. She'll settle this silly debate once and for all."

I gulped and set the tray down on the coffee table in front of Mortimer, purposefully positioning myself between him and Ellie who sat cross-legged on the floor on the opposite side. "I don't even know what this is about."

"Trust me," Rosemary said next to me. "You don't want to know."

I side-glanced Ellie's business partner in the funeral home a few towns over. The soft glow of her flush accentuated the deep tone of her skin and brought out the sharpness of her features, polishing them to a knife-like edge. Her long hair shone with an unnatural glint that often made me wonder if she was also a fae. She wasn't, of course, but if anyone came too close to being a paranormal in the group, it was Rosemary. She was simply too perfect.

I smiled. "I'm sure that's true."

"She's got a point," Finn agreed, his deep voice booming through my bones. "Run while you have the chance."

Chuckling, I handed him a cup of tea and worked to ignore the electricity that sparked along my skin when the tips of our fingers touched. There was something about Finn that made it difficult to walk away from him despite the fact that I had no business getting involved with anyone right now. Especially not a human. And especially since *he* was in town.

My smile faltered and a grimace took its place.

"Not to change the subject but what's everyone reading?" Rosemary asked.

I almost cackled. Changing the subject was exactly what she planned to do. I eyed the funeral director gleefully. *I see you, Rosemary Singh. Well played.*

"Well, before I was so rudely interrupted, I was making my way through the fascinating history of garment creation," Mortimer said.

Ellie scoffed. "Only you would find that fascinating."

"And what did you decide on?" Mortimer asked.

The young woman waved a book in the air like she was signaling a ship from the shores of an island. "If you must know, I found a book on coding." She glared at me. "I didn't take you for a computer geek."

"I'm not," I replied. "That one must have belonged to the previous director."

Ellie's eyes sparked with interest. "How long have you run this place?"

"Years," I said. "It was the one place that felt like home when I first moved to Orchard Hollow. It called to me. Luckily, the previous director was desperate to retire so he took me under his wing. I owe my life to that man."

"Where did you live before again?"

Saliva pooled in my mouth and I averted my eyes, needing to collect myself before I let too many of my secrets spill out. That was one thing I didn't enjoy about living in this realm—the lies. I loved my new group of friends but there was no way in Fairy I could ever tell them the truth of who I was. And it wasn't only because they were human and would likely have me committed.

The fae were a secretive bunch and since there were no others in this realm that I knew about, there was a good chance I'd put a target on my back if anyone was to find out we existed. The paranormals in this town were fairly docile, especially the witches and werewolves. It was the vampires and warlocks that I worried about. Since their powers stemmed directly from a power source—blood and the moon in this case—there was no telling what some would be willing to do with my magic. Drain me for it on a good day, I bet. Not that all vamps and warlocks were power-hungry enough to kill, though I did hear my fair share of stories to be wary of them.

It was in everyone's best interests that I kept my mouth shut.

My gaze flicked to Theo sleeping on the windowsill. Besides, who would deliver the changeling's daily doses of whipped cream if I was dead?

I opened my mouth to divert the question but didn't get a chance to speak before there was a loud knock on the front door. My lips pressed into a thin line. *Who could that be?*

"Do you have an appointment today?" Finn asked.

I shook my head. "Not at all. I'll go see who it is."

Dashing out of the room, I sucked in a deep breath of relief and darted for the entrance. A dread settled in the base of my stomach as I approached. My magic swirled in my veins and I could feel its power at the tips of my fingers.

What is going on?

Taking in a few more meditative breaths, I rolled my shoulders and swung the door open. My heart stopped beating instantly.

Standing before me, the Shadow Court Prince took up almost the entire doorway. His long dark hair fell down in restless waves and his wide eyes studied me with the precision of a hunter. Rhyven. The fae prince that followed me into this realm after I narrowly escaped with my life. Also known as my ex-fiancé.

Oh, yes. Did I forget to mention? The reason I was on Earth was because I ran from an arranged engagement my father made in some sad attempt to gain more power for the Summer Court. My life was a sordid tale of a fairy in hiding and one that was running right off the rails now that Rhyven was here.

I ground my teeth into a fine pulp. "What are you doing here?" I hissed out.

"Hello to you too," the prince replied. The smirk on his face made my belly clench. Rhyven held up a paper bag with the logo of a coffee cup in space on it. "Have you been to Bean Me Up? Quirky little place. I was told they have the best scones and thought we might enjoy them together."

I shook my head. "A witch owns the place," I told him. "The scones are probably spelled. And now is not a great time."

Never is a good time for you.

"Do you have company over?"

The way he asked the question, with a hint of jealousy in his voice, made me more pleased than I should have been. Sure, Rhyven showed up out of the blue to convince me to fall for him fair and square when I assumed he was here to kill me, but it still didn't mean I trusted the man. No one in the Shadow Court was to be trusted. Especially not the prince. Yet, it was nice to see him squirm for a change. This was the most vulnerable I had seen Rhyven in his entire life and I had known the fae since we were tiny fairy children.

I crossed my arms defiantly. "Work associates," I said. Technically, not a lie. "And I would prefer not to have to explain why there's a fae prince on my doorstep."

I started to shut the door but Rhyven slipped his foot in, blocking it from closing. He shoved the bag through the slit, his brows rising. "I meant what I said, Lyra. I will do whatever it takes to convince you to come home on your own terms," he purred. Then, pushing the bag in further. "You should definitely eat these. I may have snuck one on the way over and they truly are phenomenal."

With a turn of the heel, he stomped down the stairs and down the driveway, leaving me with the scones and a full blast of frustration to deal with. As Rhyven's form grew smaller, I briefly wondered how he got all the way up the cliff-side road and to the manor. There was no car parked in the driveway, and I didn't hear a taxi pull up. Though knowing Rhyven, he probably flew here without a care in the world. Something told me that staying under the radar was not as important to the Shadow Prince as it was to me.

Frowning, I opened the bag and inhaled. The sweet

smell of blueberries pierced my senses and I crumbled the bag closed with a frustrated groan. "Fairy damn you, Rhyven. These smell amazing."

A scream tore through the manor at my back. The bag of scones tore from my grip, tumbling to the ground and landing with a heavy thud. I twirled around, shutting the door with a definitive click behind me as I raced down the hallway toward the living room where the scream had come from. Sweat pooled at the base of my neck and rolled down my back. My pulse thundered between my ears. As I drew closer to the room and the Wardens, I could only think of one thing.

Who for the love of Fairy died this time?

Chapter Two

"What happened? Is everyone all right?"

I burst into the room so fast I had to use the carpet in the center of the living room to break my speed. My feet skidded across it, toes catching the fibers a little too eagerly. I teetered then went flying head forward, breaking my fall by mere inches by scraping the wallpaper with my nails. If I wasn't so worried, I'd have been embarrassed.

Before me, Ellie glared at the cellphone she clutched in her hand, beads of perspiration collecting on her forehead.

My stomach sank into my heels. She must have received terrible, life-altering news while I was shooing Rhyven off.

I closed the space between us, resting a hand on her shoulder. "What's going on?"

"Quite literally nothing," Mortimer drawled from the couch.

"But I heard Ellie scream," I said, confused. "It sounded serious."

Hands still holding her phone, Ellie batted her lashes at me from behind her wide frames but said nothing.

"Oh, for heaven's sake, Ellie, stop the theatrics," Rosemary scolded her friend. "It is not the end of the world."

A few more eyelash twitches and Ellie finally found her voice. "Not the end of the world?" She shook her head. "You don't know my Aunt Dot."

I took a step back and looked around the room for any clue as to what I missed. Was Ellie's aunt in trouble? And if she was, why were we standing around here discussing it and not rushing off to help her? The more I waited for someone to explain, the less I understood what I had walked into. It was moments such as this that reminded me how new I was to the group. I used to feel a similar way when I first came through the portal into this realm—completely out of place. But I figured out my place among the humans, and supernaturals, in Orchard Hollow. I would do the same with my new friends in time.

I swallowed the lump in my throat and turned to Finn. "What am I missing here?"

"Ellie is being overly dramatic," he replied with a warm smile. "Nothing new there."

"Excuse you! If it's no big deal, why don't you deal with her nonsense?" Ellie rebutted.

Finn chuckled. "Because she's your aunt. I have my own family to avoid, thank you very much."

"Nice excuse."

I shook my head, still entirely in the dark. "Let's take a step back," I suggested. "Why don't you tell what happened to your aunt and why it has you so riled up?"

Ellie huffed out a frustrated breath. She pocketed her phone then leaned against the wall, crossing her arms in aggravation. Her eyes met mine, flashing briefly.

"Dot is a nightmare to deal with," she said. "She has an avid imagination and is in constant need of attention. It is never-ending. And since my cousin lives across the country, I'm the one that has to deal with her."

I blinked rapidly, starting to realize that Mortimer may have been right about the situation. Ellie really did seem to blow things out of proportion.

"Only last week I had to tear apart her attic wall because she was convinced a family of raccoons had moved in there," Ellie went on. "There were no raccoons. Obviously. But guess who then had to help her patch up the hole? She is so dramatic!"

I bit my bottom lip and kept my lips sealed before I told Ellie that the trait definitely ran in the family. Swallowing a laugh, I watched the young woman fuss with the straps of her suspenders, snapping them over and over again as she fumed.

"Was there another raccoon sighting?" I asked.

"Worse," Ellie said with a sigh. "Dot has it in her head that the owner of a yarn shop where her crochet club meets is being extorted and wants me to help with tracking the so-called villain through his e-mails. Unfortunately, someone made the mistake of telling her that I am tech-inclined and she thinks I'm the answer. As though I can do anything with that ancient machine they have in the shop. The thing is a thousand years old so even if Dot wasn't imagining a crime where there isn't one, I doubt I'd be able to track any information. I don't even think Tangled Skeins has a website, let alone online banking."

I chuckled under my breath. "Tangled Skeins. Cute."

My gaze flicked to the grandfather clock in the corner of the room. The schedule was fairly free for the remainder of the afternoon with only one appointment from someone interested in securing a burial plot for his grandfather later in the evening. With the way things were going, the book club would be nothing but arguments if I didn't separate Mortimer and Ellie. And I had never been inside a yarn shop before so the idea of learning more about crocheting and possibly picking up a new hobby was intriguing.

Mostly, I wanted to get out of the house and go somewhere my mind wasn't constantly drawn back to the Fairy-blasted portal I accidentally opened and Rhyven's unwelcomed visit. My stomach growled at the thought of the scones he'd dropped off.

"Tell you what," I told Ellie. "If you're not opposed to stopping for lunch on the way, I can come with you to check out the shop so you have an excuse to leave if it's a dead end."

Ellie's brows hiked up to the top of her forehead. "Really? You don't mind?"

I shook my head.

"Are you sure you have time for that?" Finn asked.

I tipped my head in Mortimer's direction then widened my eyes so he got the clue. Luckily, Finn was a quick one and could read me instantly. He nodded, smiling.

"Well, have fun you two," he said, crossing his legs, opening the book he was studying back to the page he left it on. "We'll hold the fort here until you get back. I'm sure Mortimer is dying to tell us all about the stitches they used on pants during the Renaissance."

The old man sat up straighter on the couch, his teeth

splitting into an eager smile. "A running backstitch was quite common."

"See?" Finn asked. "We can have just as much fun too."

Laughing, I grabbed Ellie's shoulders and led her out of the living room before she could change her mind. At this point, I'd have done anything to get out of listening to Mortimer recount sewing facts and, I had to admit, I was very interested in seeing what Aunt Dot had to say. She sounded to be an even bigger personality than Ellie was, and I couldn't wait to see the two women together.

Tangled Skeins sat at the end of a narrow street, tucked between a closed-down storefront and an old-fashioned bookstore. The front window, framed by white-painted trim, was an adorable display of colorful yarn cakes stacked in neat little pyramids, their fibers catching the afternoon light and making the colors appear that much brighter. A hand-lettered chalkboard on the sidewalk read: *Come in and stitch awhile!* in curling script, and beneath it, someone had added *Crochet Club meets today!* in bright pink chalk.

The door had a little brass bell above it, and when we stepped inside, it gave a loud chime, announcing our arrival. The scent of wool and lavender sachets welcomed me as soon as I walked in. Skirting around me, Ellie led the way, clearly familiar with the place, but I took my time to snoop around. The place was mesmerizing.

Inside, the shop was a cozy maze of shelves and cubbies, all overflowing with yarn in every imaginable shade. Skeins of hand-dyed merino wool hung in bundles of spun magic, each one created of unique swirls of color that reminded me of watercolor paintings. Baskets held balls of soft alpaca and cotton blends, their labels neatly arranged to show the details of the yarn for anyone interested in purchasing it. Against one wall, a wooden rack displayed an array of hooks and needles, from sleek metal to handcrafted wooden ones with ornate handles. It was all so new to me that I couldn't help but gawk at each tool, wondering what one would use it to create.

Near the center of the shop, a small group of women sat in a circle of mismatched chairs, their hands busy with projects. The crochet club. A hum of conversation from the group was punctuated by occasional laughter that was contagious. Though I had never picked up a crochet hook, I wanted nothing more than to join them. The tea cart that sat nearby, hosting a pot of freshly brewed tea and a plate of shortbread cookies, probably had a lot to do with that.

I smiled, taking a deep breath of the wool-scented air. The yarn shop was the kind of place that made you want to stay for longer than you intended to.

Perhaps I would.

"I only have ten minutes and then I have to run!" Ellie said loudly. She made her way to one woman in the group in particular, an older lady with jet-black hair, a bright purple knitted sweater, and glasses that matched Ellie's on her pointed nose. "No time to waste."

Maybe I wouldn't be staying as long as I thought ...

The woman Ellie towered over smiled warmly and lowered her crochet hook, dragging her project—an oversized square made of a rainbow of colors—down to her lap. She flattened out the piece and inspected it before putting everything aside to stand up. As she did, she seemed to have doubled in size like a giant emerging from a cocoon. One second I was looking at a small figure fiddling with yarn and the next I watched Ellie's form cower and shrink standing beside this tall Amazonian warrior. The woman continued to smile as she placed both hands on Ellie's shoulders.

"Ellie, dear," she said in a voice reminiscent of a bird singing. "You rush around too much. Exactly like your mom."

Ellie scoffed. "I know, Aunt Dot. We are busy women. Now what's this about extortion?"

"Shush!" Dot scolded. She pulled Ellie away from the group and toward the front counter, her voice lowering a few octaves as she passed me. "We don't want to raise a panic. I promised Lillian I wouldn't make a big deal out of it."

"Too late for that," Ellie countered.

As they stepped around me, I caught Dot's gaze, and it hovered on me for a moment too long before she blinked away. She turned a wide, prominent shoulder, a clear sign the woman did not trust me with the information she was about to give her niece. I was about to walk away and spend time perusing the yarn shelves when Ellie's arm yanked me toward them.

"Aunt Dot, this is my friend Lyra. She has an even busier schedule than me, so if you wouldn't mind filling us in so we can speed this up?"

Dot shook her head in frustration then glanced at me again. "Nice to meet you, Lyra. I hope you have a tad more patience than my niece." With a grimace, she pointed to the aforementioned computer Ellie had sniped about. "I tried to get the blasted thing to turn on, but I had no luck all morning. Maybe you two can give it a shot and see what you can find out."

"Where's Lillian? It's her shop," Ellie said. "Shouldn't she be here?"

"She had to run out. Supply run, I believe. But I can help with whatever you need."

I looked at the dusty old computer atop the register counter, a frown tugging at my lips. The beige casing had yellowed with time and a faint hum of an outdated fan blended with the sound of the conversation from the crochet club behind me. The screen flickered as though it could feel me watching it only to go out again.

The thing was on its last legs.

Ellie must have had the same realization. She set her jaw and scratched her forehead to release the lines of worry gathering there. "Dot," she said through clenched teeth. "How about we start with why you think Lillian is being extorted and then I can try to bring that beast back to life."

The crocheting aunt looked over her shoulder and pressed her lips together into a tight line.

"There's a gentleman," she started. "Goes by the name of Brighton Glass. He's had his eye on the shop for years. It's a great location so who could blame him, right?"

I nodded.

Ellie frowned.

"Anyhow, he's been pressuring Lillian to sell the place for ages. And I think it took a real turn lately."

At this, Ellie's eyes widened and she paused, looking

at me then back to her aunt. "Why do you say that? Did you see him do something?"

"Not that I know of," Dot admitted. She lowered her chin, her eyes narrowing as she gazed at us through bushy brows. "But Lillian has been acting all sorts of squirrely and I know that's the reason. I mean, what else could it be?"

In front of me, Ellie's arms shot up in the air then smacked down on her thighs with a loud clap. "Literally anything else, Dot! That's why you called me over? Is there any actual proof that your friend was being extorted?"

"That's why I called you," Dot rebutted. She pointed to the computer again. "So you can find proof that I can take to the police since Lillian is obviously too afraid to do it herself."

Ellie's brows creased so hard her skin turned red between them. "First of all, that thing needs to be put out to pasture. Second, I can't break into the online files of a business without permission. It's illegal."

"Is that what you're fussing over?" Dot waved her hand in front of Ellie's face dismissively. "If that's the case, let's give Lillian a call so she can tell you herself. I'm sure there will be no trouble at all for you to take a quick looksee."

At this, Ellie's shoulders dropped, and I instantly

knew my friend was trapped. Dot struck me as the kind of woman that was impossible to say no to. Especially if she was anything like her niece.

Ellie rubbed her eyes furiously then opened them wide to look at me. "Think you can hang out for a second? This won't take long."

"Take all the time you need," I replied. "I'll go chat with the club. Their projects look really fun!"

I left the women to fumble at the counter and made my way to the center of the shop and the busy ladies sitting there. The sound of hushed conversation got louder as I approached and I slowed my pace, hovering near the chairs like Theo hovered near a bag of opened salami. My eyes scanned the women's quick fingers as they flicked yarn over this way and that way to form neat little rows. It was mesmerizing.

"Care to join us?" one of the women asked. Her heavily sprayed blonde curls barely moved as she flicked her project to the side and scooted one chair over and closer to her friend, leaving a space for me to sit closer to the side table.

I winced. "I don't crochet," I admitted, stepping forward. "At least, I've never tried to."

"That's nothing to be ashamed of." The second woman chuckled. Her warm hazel eyes focused on me intently. "I'm Sylvia and this one here is Edna. Half the people who shop here can't crochet to save their lives so don't stress over it. Most come for the gossip."

A few chuckles rippled through the women before Edna blew out a stiff huff, motioning to the chair she freed up and then focusing on the stitches in her lap.

I slid into the open chair, my hands folded in my lap neatly.

"So," Sylvia said, nudging a teacup toward me, "we're working on a group project right now—a crochet tapestry inspired by the history of the town. A little bit of the past stitched into every square."

She placed a large blanket in front of me that I was drawn to immediately. The colors reminded me of the flowers I grew in the garden—all sorts of shades that I couldn't help but stare at. I traced my fingers over one of the finished squares with a smile.

"That's mine," Sylvia said, her voice brimming with pride. "It's based on an old crochet pattern I found at an estate sale. Vintage—possibly over a hundred years old."

"You're *still* claiming that?" Edna's sharp voice cut through the warmth of the shop. "That pattern belonged to my great-grandmother. I've told you before, Sylvia—it came from my family."

Sylvia rolled her eyes. "We've been over this. I found it fair and square."

Edna's gaze sharpened, like she wanted to say something else, but then she only smiled. "Let's not scare the girl right off the bat, or she might go by the wayside as Betty did."

"Who's Betty?" I asked before I could stop myself.

"A new member we are all eager to meet. She was supposed to come by for a crochet session several times now, but something always came up," Sylvia replied. "And don't listen to Edna. She's only bitter over, well, everything. We've been running the club for over a decade now and *some people* are not great with welcoming newcomers."

Edna harrumphed. "I'm not the one who hasn't shown up to a single meeting yet."

"Give Betty a break," Sylvia said. "You know young people these days."

"I know one should not sign up for a club they don't wish to attend."

Edna raised a single thin brow my way and I found myself sinking into the deep cushion of the chair. I gulped, my mouth suddenly dry and my throat uncannily full. My gaze rolled past the women to the counter where Ellie appeared to be arguing with Dot while simultaneously attempting to revive the relic of a computer on the counter. My chest tightened.

I focused my attention on Edna, holding my palm out. "You know what? I would love to try my hand at crocheting," I announced.

"Are you sure?" Edna asked. "It takes a while to get the hang of it."

My eyes crinkled as I grabbed the crochet hook and ball of yarn she was already handing over. "I'm a fast learner," I said. "And I have the feeling I might be here for longer than anticipated."

Chapter Three

The clatter of crochet hooks and conversation filled the front room of Tangled Skeins: the weekly crochet meeting was in full swing. I sat in the mismatched circle of chairs surrounding a table brimming with yarn cakes in every hue, half-finished shawls, steaming mugs of tea, and the occasional plate of date squares. Around me, the women continued to gossip and crochet, a winning combination of activities it appeared. Even Dot left Ellie to her own devices with the computer and picked up a project bag.

Nothing got in between the club and their hooks.

Well, perhaps nothing but my incessant questions.

I scrunched my forehead as I studied the mess of yarn in my lap. "I think I missed a stitch," I announced, frowning.

"I'd say," Dot replied.

She reached over and held out her hand, beckoning me to surrender the disgrace of a granny square over. Working her own crochet hook with nimble fingers, Ellie's aunt tugged and pulled and pulled and tugged as she attempted to save my first attempt at crocheting. To my complete astonishment, the clump of yarn was slowly taking form, and within minutes, the shape of a square began to emerge. My mouth flew open.

"You are ridiculously good at this," I said.

Dot smiled, her lips thinning out as she handed the project back to me. "You'll get the hang of it, dear. Everyone always does." She pointed to the square I held. "Remember to yarn over and not under, it'll make the stitches less tight."

"Unless you're making toys," Sylvia said.

"Or like a tighter row," Edna added.

I shook my head and made mental notes of their advice, cataloguing it with the rest of the instructions I tried to infuse into my brain as I learned the craft. If I had known how difficult crocheting was, I would have reconsidered joining the group today. Or used magic to help me, not that I knew how to do that. My fairy skills were tied to the earth, not matters of craft. Besides, even the skills I did have were wonky at best lately.

Taking a few more stabs with my hook, I grimaced when the square started to tangle again. There was a good chance I would never learn. Perhaps I should have stuck to gardening, a thing I actually knew a lot about.

I was about to ask Dot for help again when the bell hanging over the front door rang and two women strolled into the shop. My eyes widened at the sight of them. The first woman waved at the group like she had seen them a million times over then marched straight for the front counter. Her long red hair swayed behind her as she walked and brushed against the handknit cardigan she wore. As she approached the counter, she looked between Ellie and Dot, her lips pressing into a thin line. Without a word, she dropped the large bags she dragged in and began to unpack skeins of yarn onto the counter.

That must be Lillian Everwood, I thought. The shop owner.

Peeling my gaze from the counter, I concentrated on the second woman to enter the shop—one I already knew fairly well.

"Hello Maggie," I told the town librarian when her eyes met mine.

Maggie's shoulders stiffened and it took her a second to collect herself. I didn't doubt she was as surprised to see me here as I was, after all, it wasn't often you'd find your local undertaker in a yarn shop. But it also was as odd to see her here. Maggie made it a point to follow death around almost as closely as I had and it was my profession for Fairy's sake! Since she'd started writing that dreadful true crime book years ago, she was always lurking at crime scenes and visiting funeral homes. It was how I met her in the first place.

It was also likely how she met Mortimer and started ... Well, whatever it was they had going on. Those two had a love hate relationship I didn't think I'd ever understand.

The librarian eyed me with curiosity then forced a smile, making her thick foundation crack and her glasses ride up on the bridge of her nose. She strolled my way, plopping down into an empty seat with an exasperated sigh.

"Miss Moore," she cooed, her gaze narrowed on the yarn monstrosity in my lap. "I didn't realize you enjoyed crocheting."

I chuckled. "That makes two of us. But I'm only here with a friend, not joining any clubs.

"For now ..." Sylvia teased.

"And Lyra is fine," I added.

"Oh hush!" Maggie told Sylvia. "I'm certain Lyra has better things to do with her time than spend it with us. Like run the funeral home."

A collective gasp ran through the group.

"You're the mysterious funeral home director?" Sylvia asked. "The one from up in the cliffs?"

I nodded and tried to swallow, my throat suddenly bone-dry.

Before I could clear it, Edna squeezed my arm so tight I almost yelped. I turned to see the woman's pale blue eyes widen in intrigue. Her clammy fingers clutched my skin as she said, "That place is haunted, you know."

"Edna, stop your babbling nonsense," Maggie scolded.

Beside her, Sylvia's bubbly laugh pierced through the shop. "If anyone would know, it's you," she told her friend. "If it was, you'd have written all about it in your little novel."

"I write true crime, you hobbit," Maggie argued. "Not fairy tales."

Leaning into the warmth of the chair, I sat back and watched the women playfully argue. They continued to crochet as they did, never so much as dropping a stitch. Even Maggie produced from her quilted purse an intricate sweater that was the color of red apples and looked so lush I could hug it. The three struck me as the type of friends who were more akin to family. A little like the Grim Wardens were. At least, their banter was quite on point.

I watched Maggie pinch Edna in between stitches and laughed.

So much like the Wardens.

Focusing my attention on my own project, I creased my brow and attempted to disassemble the mess I had made earlier. No matter what I did, it seemed I dug myself further into a hole. The knots got knottier to the point that I couldn't even stab my hook into the tangled mess. I sighed, placing the creation from Hell to the side before anyone noticed.

"Ladies," Sylvia said out of nowhere. "I believe I've found something rather special."

Curiosity bloomed instantly, hooks stilled mid-loop, and the group leaned closer, myself included. Sylvia, with the air of someone unveiling the final clue in a Victorian mystery, carefully licked her full lips and smiled sneakily.

"A vintage pattern," she explained. "Edwardian, judging by the terminology. Tucked inside an old gardening manual I picked up at the estate sale on Carrycut Lane."

Gasps and murmurs circled the room. I peered above the women's heads at the counter where Lillian Everwood stopped her unpacking and was eagerly listening to what Sylvia had to say. Whatever the deal was with this pattern, it had everyone's interest. Even mine and I hadn't the foggiest clue what any of it meant.

"I believe," Sylvia added, eyes glinting, "that this pattern is truly special."

That earned her a pause in the murmur, and silence fell like a dropped stitch.

"Special how?" Maggie asked.

Sylvia gave a small, satisfied smile. "I won't say more for now. But there's more to this design than meets the eye. The way the scalloped edge is done backwards is in itself a feast for the eyes. Not to mention the color changes around the added rose designs ... In fact—" she patted the purse at her feet "—I believe it's so special I refuse to part with it."

Before anyone could press further, Edna Furlow made a strangled sound from her seat near the tea cart. Her cheeks flushed crimson, and she leaned forward, finger pointed like a knitting needle mid-thrust.

"That's *my great-grandmother's* pattern!" she hissed out. "How many times do I have to spell it out for you?"

Sylvia's smile froze.

"I beg your pardon?" she said sharply.

Edna surged to her feet. "Mildred Furlow. She used to make lace collars and trims for the ladies of the St. Gloria Garden Society. That's *her* scalloped edging. I've seen it on her pieces a hundred times. That pattern was in her journal, and it was stolen from her house years ago when—when we had that break-in!"

"You are being ridiculous," Sylvia warned. "I bought the pattern fair and square. Besides, that is a seashell edge. Not scalloped! You're delusional."

The shop grew edges, sharp with confusion and tension.

Sylvia stood up, clutching her pearl necklace protectively. "I assure you, Edna, I found this in a book at a sale. I have the receipt. Are you accusing me of theft?"

"I'm saying that pattern was stolen from my family. I don't know how it ended up at that sale, but it's not yours to flaunt."

Maggie, caught between them, shot me a panicked glance. I swallowed the lump in my throat, gaze darting around the room for a distraction. If I could get the two to calm down, we could stop a fight from breaking out. I didn't know how far the women would go over a crochet pattern, but both were holding their hooks like weapons, and I was not willing to find out. To make matters worse, Dot had completely abandoned Ellie and was now watching from the sidelines, her eyes animated with excitement. I was beginning to gather that the group was prone to arguments like this.

Catching Ellie's eyes, I nudged my chin to the door and asked, "How's that computer looking?"

Ellie blinked, then nodded.

"Nothing yet." She turned to Lillian who barely made eye contact, her focus solely on the women in the center of the shop. "Think you can spare me the headache of going through all this data and tell my aunt that there is nothing to worry about? She is not going to rest until she hears it from your lips."

"Oh, for heaven's sake. Sylvia, for the last time, the shop is not being sold," Lillian said. Her voice was soft but assertive and I realized this wasn't the first time she had entertained Ellie's aunt and her wild ideas. "I can handle my own business."

That seemed to do the trick. Sylvia peeled her angry gaze from Edna and turned it on Lillian. She spun around, forcibly shoving her shoulders out to block Edna's view of the counter.

Geez. The woman could hold a grudge.

"I was only trying to help," she said sweetly.

"I know," Lillian said. She placed the last of the yarn on the counter and waved her friend over. "Now come look at this. I found the most brilliant merino at the dyer that's going to look amazing on the cardigan you wanted to crochet. Come feel it. It's soft as a feather."

As Sylvia sauntered to the counter, leaving Edna behind, I couldn't help but wonder what I witnessed a moment ago. At the circle, teacups clanged as Maggie refilled the teas and the sound of hooks swooshing in yarn took over the shop once more. And yet I couldn't shake the feeling that something was amiss. Lillian was much too quick to dismiss Sylvia's theory and the way her smile was pinched made me think she was holding back.

There were secrets in this shop. Buried behind skeins of yarn and tucked into the shelves. That I was sure of. Then again, what place in a small town didn't have a secret or two? Especially a town full of paranormals.

I lifted my nose and sniffed the air to confirm there was no magic around to be on the safe side. Leaving the women, I walked to join Ellie by the front door. I could tell she was more than ready to get out of here. As if on cue, my stomach rumbled.

"Time for that lunch," Ellie said. "Finally."

I smiled, waving goodbye to everyone before opening the front door. The warm air from the street drifted inside and the smell of pastries baking somewhere nearby made my stomach muscles clench. Before leaving, my eyes caught on Edna and the scowl plastered on her face.

I shook my head.

Whatever the mystery of the crochet pattern was, it was not important. If I didn't eat soon, I might pass out. I followed Ellie out of the shop and walked down the street to the nearest bakery. As the distance between me and Tangled Skeins grew, I couldn't help but glance over my shoulder. It was a cute shop despite the turn the afternoon took, and I made a mental point to return later. Maybe it was time for a new hobby after all.

Chapter Four

"**M**aybe you should join the club. Something to do other than poke around dead people all day," drawled the cat as he perched on the side of the window sill in my bedroom.

His fluffy grey tail swung lazily from side to side and the sunlight hit it just enough to make the furry haze around him appear like it was glowing. I cast a down-turned smile his way. "I don't poke around dead people," I said grimly. "I run a funeral home. There is a difference."

"Or so you say," Theo argued.

"Besides," I continued, not letting the cat annoy me any further. "I don't exactly have time for another hobby. Not with everything going on here. And you wouldn't say these things if you saw the abomination I created in my short time with the club. Trust me, I was not made for crocheting."

Theo's eyes narrowed slightly and for a second, I thought he was going to be mean again, but this time the cat surprised me. He licked his paw once. Twice. Rested it on the window sill and looked at me with an expression that was almost akin to concern. "Have you given any more thought as to what you're going to do about the Shadow Prince?"

I frowned. The truth was, I hadn't given Rhyven any thought at all since the scone incident. Having the Shadow Prince around was nothing short of frustrating, but if I was honest, he wasn't my biggest concern. My head was continuously trapped inside that strange portal I opened. In that bizarre land covered in snow and ice. Where did the portal lead? It wasn't any realm I had ever seen, and it wasn't anywhere on Earth that was for certain. Nor in Fairy. Even the Winter Court did not look quite as desolate and barren. No, this was something else. Someplace way beyond my understanding and knowledge. And someplace that I simply couldn't get out of my head.

I even dreamt about it last night.

After I got back from Tangled Skeins, I was hit by the type of exhaustion that I hadn't felt in years. It was as though my bones were giving up and fading out of my body. Running away to avoid any more work than I might inflict on them. I ended up pushing to later all the paperwork that I had to do for Mr. Myers' Sunday service and fell asleep before my head even hit the pillow. I was hoping for a good night's rest to clear my mind and all the nerves that had bottled up inside my body. Yet that was not in the cards. Instead of a good night's rest I got the fresh reminder of my wretched magic powers and the chaos they could create. I dreamt of blizzards and snowfalls so hard they buried cities. I dreamt of shadowy monsters hiding in corners and lurking in dead trees. I dreamt of death.

It was why when Theo burst into my room before the sun rose this morning asking for a bowl of cream, I didn't scold him like I usually did. Instead, I tore myself from my sweat, soaked sheets and followed the cat downstairs eagerly. Watching a changeling down a carton of cream was a way better distraction than anything my mind could have conjured.

I glanced out the window of the manor and into the backyard where my garden stood in full bloom. This season I decided to use my powers in a way that felt safe and in the way that I knew couldn't cause any problems. Which was to say I used it in the garden. There was a new row of tulips that bloomed overnight and gardenias filled every empty corner. The roses I had grown so proud of had multiplied to the point that I could smell them even through the small crack in the window. They were still in the strange shade of purple they had turned to, though. Another quirk of my magic I was yet to figure out. But they were beautiful, nonetheless.

I smiled at the sudden warmth hugging my heart and brought the teacup I held to my lips to take a long sip of the steeped Earl Grey inside. "You know what?" I told the changeling. "I think, for the first time since I arrived in this realm, I am not going to let anything bother me. Not even the Prince of the Shadow Court."

"You don't say," Theo remarked.

"I do say, indeed," I teased. "I have to admit I don't trust Rhyven as far as I can throw him. And I definitely don't believe him when he says he has no ulterior intentions other than to make me come home with him willingly. But I don't have the mental capacity right now for any added stress."

"You know, you might not be so stressed if you hadn't decided to join an undertaker society that seems to really enjoy being around dead people."

A heightened laugh burst from my lips. "Theo. Being around dead people is literally their entire job."

"Yes, I am aware. Which is why it is incredibly odd that they choose to bring more death into their lives by chasing after these cases." The changeling's gaze burned into me. "And you appear to be very keen on following in the same footsteps."

I was about to tell the cat to shove his opinions where the fae suns didn't shine but before I could open my mouth the downstairs doorbell rang, making me jump in surprise. My eyes locked on Theo, a questioning look crossing my face.

"I thought you had the day off," the cat said.

I groaned. "I was supposed to. There was only a little bit of paperwork left to do and then I was planning to rightfully spend the remainder of the afternoon doing absolutely nothing." My stomach churned with worry. *I wonder who that could be.*

Throwing my legs over the bed reluctantly, I dragged myself from the cocoon of pillows I'd created, set the teacup down, and made my way downstairs. Around me, the burgundy wallpaper seemed to close in with every step I took toward the front door. I felt the air in my lungs seep out. My ribs pressed in on my heart as the threat of dealing with whatever was on the other side of the doorway took over.

I really needed a vacation.

Perhaps something I could look into. I hadn't stepped foot outside of Orchard Hollow since I arrived ages ago; stricken by the fear of being discovered. But now that the one person I was hoping to avoid was right here in town, it wouldn't be the worst idea to go away for a while. If only to dip my toes in the ocean and catch a much-needed tan.

I reached the front door and rolled my shoulders down. As I pulled the door open, the glower on my face vanished and my lips turned up at the corners.

"Finn!" I exclaimed. "What a nice surprise. What brings you by?"

Standing on my front porch and looking as handsome as ever, Finn O'Malley shrugged awkwardly. His eyes twinkled and the creases around them made my legs turn to liquid. He raked calloused fingers through his messy brown hair, the leather of his bomber jacket straining under the pull of his bicep muscles. "I brought you some tea from the Whistling Kettle," he said, holding out a small paper bag. "Edith said you were due for a refill when I stopped by there on my way to work, so I figured I'd swing by to drop it off personally. Gave me an excuse to see you."

I sucked in a deep breath and the fabric of my blouse tightened against my chest. Never in a million fairy years would I have imagined that I'd be in this position. Dating was never at the forefront of my mind; thus I never paid much attention to it. Even in Fairy I kept mostly to myself, though that could be due to the arranged marriage hanging over my head. But even since I escaped my home and came here, my love life has been, as Theo put it, dusty. And yes, I knew it was because I had to stay in hiding, not to draw attention to myself, but truthfully that was likely an excuse I used.

There were plenty of paranormals that I could have gone out with in this town. Most had their own secrets to keep—I would be in good company. But I never followed through, and I wasn't about to try to dissect my confusing psyche with Finn standing in front of me.

I plastered on a faltering smile and took the bag from him, inhaling the rich aroma of the tea inside. My shoulders drooped in relief and a sigh escaped my lips.

"That good, huh?"

I shook my head. "Better. Thank you for bringing this by. I hope you're not going to be late for work because of me."

"Not at all. That's the beauty of being the director of a morgue—the schedule is fairly relaxed. Not many emergencies in my workplace."

"I'm sure we can all agree to that," I joked.

Awkwardness stretched between us, both of us staring but not saying anything else. We were yet to discuss our interrupted date that was never rescheduled, though it wasn't for the lack of Finn trying. He hinted at going out again several times, but I always brushed him off. How could I possibly give Finn my full attention with Rhyven popping into my head like an annoying thorn? No, if I wished to go on another date with Finn, it would be when the mess of my life was finally straightened out. It was what he deserved.

"Lyra?"

I shook my head. *Blast. How long was I out of it?*

"Sorry," I said. A heat clawed its way up my neck. "Would you like to come in?"

Finn shoved his hands into his pockets, his full lips pressing into a thin line. "I wish I could, but if I don't show up at some point today, they might call the cops in. I've missed enough work in the last little while, what with the Wardens being so busy with our extracurriculars."

"I know what you mean," I agreed. "It's surprising how many cases we get to work on."

Finn scowled. "Not all that surprising if you think about it. I'm sure the rate of unsolved crimes is even higher in the cities. The police have their hands full and things fall through the cracks."

Perhaps, I thought. Or it was as Theo said. I could very well be a magnet for death. It would explain my job choice.

"Well, if you—"

My words were cut off by a deafening screech of tires. I tore my gaze from Finn and we both spun around to see rainbow-colored lights pierce the shadowy driveway. Gravel kicked up as two vehicles sped toward us. My stomach dropped into my shoes. My teeth gritted together as I watched a police car park next to Finn's vehicle, an ambulance pulling up behind it. Both had their lights on which told me they had rushed to get here. *What could be so urgent?*

I swallowed the acid rolling up into my throat and continued to watch a middle-aged officer step out of the car. Her dark hair was pulled into a low bun, and her uniform was crisp and shiny, like she had not been wearing it for long. She glanced at the ambulance over her shoulder. When she saw the back doors open, she spun back around to face the porch. The woman's green eyes narrowed on me. As she started her slow ascent up the steps to join us, I couldn't help but feel like something terrible was about to happen. Behind her, two paramedics climbed out of the ambulance and the familiar sound of a stretcher being lowered down made me freeze. *Not again,* I thought.

Another death. Another body. Another visitor to the Mistbrook Funeral Home.

The officer rubbed the bridge of her Greek nose. "Lyra Moore, I take it?" she asked, giving me a once over.

"That's me."

"I have a delivery, I'm afraid," the officer said. She extended her hand and I shook it. "My name is Officer Brimley. Pleasure to meet you, though I wish it was under better circumstances."

I frowned. "Lyra Moore. As you know," I said awkwardly. "I haven't seen you at the station before."

Then, realizing Finn was still there, I tipped my chin toward him and added, "This is Finn O'Malley. The morgue director over at Holbeck General Hospital."

"I see," the officer said. "I transferred from King City recently. Learning my ropes around here. Orchard Hollow seems like a wonderful place to live."

My eyes flicked to the stretcher. "Mostly."

Officer Brimley followed my gaze, her deep bronze skin paling slightly. She shuffled her feet and folded her arms over her chest, facing me again. "That? An accident, I'm afraid. Nothing quite so dreadful as what you're imagining."

"An accident?"

"Yes. A tragic one at that. One that could have been easily avoided." She looked down at the ground then back at me. "Though I was hoping you might do me the favor of examining the body more thoroughly."

I bristled. "How come?"

"Though it does appear to be an accident, it is a strange one," the officer explained. "I have to tell you, after my experience in the city, anything that doesn't sit quite right—I make a point to check it out. Even if it is off the books."

I was beginning to like Officer Brimley quite a bit. I had a similar philosophy when it came to life. If anything, so much as hinted at being off, I kept my guard up.

The paramedics wheeled the stretcher toward the porch, carefully lifting it up the steps. I looked at the body bag atop and the hole in my gut grew a few sizes. "Who was the victim?" I asked, genuinely intrigued.

The officer exchanged a quick glance with the paramedics before saying, "A local woman. Elderly. She passed away last night in a yarn shop. She was climbing to reach a high shelf and her foot slipped causing her to tumble and hit her head. The force of the hit was enough to kill her. As I said, a terrible and tragic accident."

I barely made out her words over the hammering in my head. Elderly woman in the yard shop? No, it couldn't be. Could it? My vision swam. I bit down on my tongue, a sudden dryness overtaking my mouth. I tried to swallow but my throat felt like it was closing up. Dots swarmed before me. I blinked them away, forcing myself to focus on the officer.

"W-what was her name?" I stammered.

Officer Brimley pulled out a small notebook and flipped it to a few pages in. "Sylvia Plumwell."

A gasp broke free of me.

"Did this happen in the Tangled Skeins yarn shop?" I asked.

The officer nodded. "You know the place?"

Unfortunately, I did.

The accident must have happened not so long after

I left. But what was Sylvia doing at the yarn shop late at night? Nausea filled the inside of my mouth. I was just with Sylvia and now ... She was gone.

My breath came out short. "May I?" I asked, pointing at the body bag.

Officer Brimley encouraged the paramedics to take a step back. Slowly, and with a hand so shaky I wasn't sure I'd be able to grab the zipper, I pulled the body bag open and peered inside. My throat constricted as I took in Sylvia's solid form before me. My eyes narrowed on the injury to her head then rolled down her body. She looked so peaceful.

My gaze paused on her throat for a brief moment before I zipped the body bag back up. Directing the paramedics through the manor, I helped them lower the stretcher down the basement stairs and place Sylvia on the empty slab in the center of the room.

"Do you want her in the refrigerated unit?" one paramedic asked. He was no older than thirty, but already had the look about him of someone who had seen more than most people his age.

I shook my head. "That's all right, I can manage. I'd like to examine her sooner rather than later."

After signing off on receiving the body I waited until the paramedics left the room before turning my attention to Sylvia. Finn was down the stairs and standing next to me in moments, eager to discuss what happened. He stood on the opposite side of the slab with an expression that was impossible to read.

"Very strange, no?"

We stared at Sylvia's body between us.

"What a terrible coincidence," Finn said. "Ellie mentioned you were with her only yesterday."

My spine uncurled and I stood straight as an arrow. "Not a coincidence," I told Finn. "And not an accident either."

"What do you mean?"

Gathering myself, I pinched the neckline of Sylvia's blouse between two fingers and pulled it down slightly to reveal a thin, red line across the skin of her neck. "Sylvia may have hit her head at that shop, but I don't think that was what killed her," I said grimly. "I think she may have been strangled."

"Why would anyone want to harm this sweet woman?"

I shivered. "I don't know," I admitted. "But I'm going to find out."

Chapter Five

Tombstones sprouted from the ground as I made my way through the Orchard Hollow cemetery toward the Starling Mausoleum that sat tucked in the back. Around me, copses of trees rustled in the light wind and birds occasionally took off from branches filling the otherwise silent space with life. My feet padded on the overgrown cobblestones that made up the winding pathways of the cemetery. As usual, I was the only soul here. Well, the only breathing one.

I made a sharp right by the old Sycamore tree and my eyes narrowed on the mausoleum in the distance. The structure was not unlike all the other structures in the cemetery, but I knew different. The Starling Mausoleum was special. Not because of the brick used to build it. And not because of the intricate carvings that made-up the facade of the building. It was what it housed that made it so remarkable.

I side-glanced to the left of the mausoleum, my brows furrowing. The portal I'd used to escape from Fairy held strong, locked as it had been for years now. A question popped into my head instantly.

If the border was closed, how did Rhyven make his way across to this realm?

I made a mental note to ask him later, not that I expected any honest answers from the fae prince. It was worth a shot, and I had to admit, he had my interest piqued. Pushing away all thoughts of Rhyven from my head, I pressed on the heavy door of the mausoleum and shoved my way inside. Speckles of dust flew around me, sparkling in the dim light falling in through the only window in the tight space. On this level of the mausoleum, there wasn't much to see, and if anyone were to walk in, they'd assume it was nothing more than the resting space for members of the Starling family long past.

But if you were one of the Grim Wardens, you'd know better.

I walked to the far end of the mausoleum, the soles of my boots tapping softly against the cold stone floor. The air was thick with the scent of damp earth and old roses, and the hush of the crypt settled around me like a second skin. I stopped in front of an unassuming wall, just another row of weather-worn bricks to anyone unfamiliar with its secret.

Drawing in a slow breath, I pressed my palm against a single, slightly darker brick, its surface smoother than the others from years of repeated touches. A moment passed in silence before a soft click echoed through the chamber, deep and mechanical—the sound of ancient gears finally turning. I jumped back instinctively as the stone groaned and shifted, the hidden doorway swinging inward with a long, mournful creak.

A spiral staircase revealed itself beyond the opening, descending into darkness that pulsed with energy. I didn't hesitate. Fear had long since learned it had no place in this part of my life. I took the first step, then another, the stone stairs cool beneath my feet and worn smooth by time. My hand grazed the wall as I descended, guiding myself downward until I stood directly beneath the mausoleum's floor, swallowed by the silence of the hidden chamber.

Before me formed another doorway, this one cracked just enough to reveal the flickering glow of light beyond. I pushed it open with a soft creak and stepped over the threshold into a space that still took my breath away, no matter how many times I'd been here.

The hidden library stretched out before me, carved into the earth and out of sight. Towering shelves lined the stone walls, heavy with tomes bound in cracked leather and fading cloth. Dust danced in the shafts of golden light filtering through the iron sconces. The air was rich with the scent of old paper and wax, an echo of the Starling family member who had once claimed this place as his personal retreat.

Now, it belonged to us: the Grim Wardens. Slightly spooky, entirely secret, and comfortably isolated from the prying ears of the living and the dead. It was the perfect place for strategy meetings and the unraveling of mysteries that the police couldn't, or wouldn't, solve.

I stepped deeper into the room, holding my breath for a moment as I soaked in the stillness. My gaze swept the shelves, trailing over rows of texts and forgotten histories. Then I smiled as my eyes landed on the large, round table in the center of the room.

"Hey, Ellie," I said, greeting the only other Warden in the place. "I figured I'd find you here."

Ellie Blackwood looked up at me from the book she read. There were dark circles under her eyes that I could see even through the reflection of her glasses, and she appeared as though she hadn't slept in days.

"Have you heard?" she asked.

I nodded. "The police delivered the body to my funeral home last night."

Ellie's eyes darkened, a storm brewing within them.

"I truly can't believe it. She was fine and now ..." She blinked rapidly. "Aunt Dot is absolutely destroyed."

I chucked off my light cardigan and hung it on the coat rack near the doorway, then made my way toward her. Sitting down across from Ellie, I placed my palms on the table and met her gaze. "There's something you should know," I said, my voice soft as a whisper. "Finn was there when they delivered the body. I know the police said there was an accident, that she fell and hit her head, but—"

"But what?" Ellie cut in.

I bit my bottom lip. "I saw marks on Sylvia's neck that might imply otherwise."

"You think she was murdered?" Ellie asked. Her eyes widened to saucers and her teeth split apart as she let out a small gasp. "By whom?"

"I'm not sure," I said. "To be honest, I'm not even sure if there was any foul play, but I have to admit the markings ... they were suspicious."

"What do you think caused them?"

I shrugged. "That's what Finn and I were trying to figure out, but without knowing what actually happened, it's impossible to tell."

Ellie looked at me questioningly. "What was she even doing there at that hour?"

"You know, I had the same question myself. Does

Sylvia usually stay late to help Lillian out with the shop?"

"Not that I know of," Ellie said. "But maybe she made an exception this time. Lillian has been under a lot of stress lately."

"Because of what's happening with her shop and the man threatening to run her out?"

Ellie bristled. "I really don't know. But things have been off in Tangled Skeins. At least in the last few times that I had visited."

"Off how?" I asked.

"The energy was different. Everybody who visits the shop is usually happy-go-lucky, you know? Mostly because that's how Lillian is. But lately, she's been on edge. Like something has been bothering her."

"Or someone," I suggested.

"Yes, or someone."

I picked at my fingernails and tried to gauge her reaction. Ellie was upset, that was for certain, but it was hard to tell if it was because of what happened to Sylvia or because of how her poor aunt was reacting to the incident. Not that I could blame her. If one of my good friends died tragically, I didn't know how I would react. I'd likely be as destroyed as Dot.

Ellie's tone deepened. "It is strange, isn't it? Not that she was there and at such a late hour but—" Ellie paused, a shadow crossing her face "—but that she died after what happened in the shop with Edna."

I swallowed the knot in my throat. Ellie's words hit the nail on the head. It was exactly what I thought when I saw Sylvia's body on the slab for the first time. I folded my arms over my chest. "You don't think there was any truth to what Edna said about her stealing the pattern?"

"I don't know what to think right now."

"Even if it was true," I continued. "Would Edna really kill one of her friends over a crochet pattern?"

A bitter laugh burst from Ellie's mouth. "You don't know these ladies, very well. I have been around that group almost my entire life and there is nothing they wouldn't do for a crochet pattern."

My stomach muscles clenched and knots formed in my throat. I knew she was joking, of course. She would have to be. Yet the way that Ellie spoke made me question if a small part of her theory was true. I didn't believe for a second Edna would kill over a pattern. However, Sylvia *did* mention the pattern being special. That it was special. Now the question remained: was it special enough to kill for?

A sudden coldness enveloped my bones and I shuddered. Perhaps there was more to the crochet club than met the eye. I didn't want to believe those sweet ladies could do anything so awful, but in my line of work, I had seen people do worse. Sometimes I couldn't help but wonder if humans were as bad as fairies. Perhaps not as ultimately brutal, yet terrible in their core, nonetheless. It would explain why the funeral home was always busy.

I glanced at Ellie, regaining control of my wayward thoughts again. "Have you tried to talk to Dot about it? To see if there was anyone that might have wanted to harm her friend?"

"Sure did," Ellie said with a scoff.

My eyebrows slanted in her direction "And?"

"She hinted that Sylvia may have gotten herself in over her head but wouldn't say with what. Even after I pushed. The thing about Dot and Sylvia that you have to know is that they weren't only crochet friends. Sylvia was my aunt's best friend since high school. They had known each other for ages. In fact, it was Sylvia who encouraged Dot to start the crochet club. They mostly ran it together and in that time, they had grown even closer, almost like sisters. If Sylvia did anything that may have caused her death, Dot would never let it slip. She'd go to her own grave protecting her friend's secrets, especially if she thought they were dark enough to end Sylvia's life."

The echo of distant voices sounded from the mausoleum and I froze. Sitting across the table from me, Ellie's eyes darted to the open door then ran around the room.

"Probably people visiting a grave," she said. "It tends to get creepy down here sometimes."

I laughed. "A secret lair beneath a mausoleum in the cemetery? Creepy? You don't say!"

The pathetic joke earned me a crooked smile from Ellie. She brushed a loose curl from her forehead and tucked it behind her ear. It fell away instantly. Ellie took off her glasses, blew hot air on the lenses and cleaned them with a corner of her black shirt.

"Anyway, sorry to be such a downer," she said. "Why are you here today?"

"To check on you," I admitted. "I wanted to see how you were holding up. As soon as I finished examining Sylvia early this morning, I thought it was best to check on you."

Ellie's eyes sparkled as she looked me over. "Thank you."

I smiled. "No need to thank me." I rested my elbows on the oak table top, placing my chin in the palms of my hands. "Are you sure you'll be all right?"

Ellie waved me off. "I'll be fine. I promised Dot I'd take her out for a coffee later. It's not a good time for her to be alone. Maybe stop by Tangled Skeins to see how the rest of the group is holding up."

"I think that's an excellent idea," I said. "I might be able to pop in and meet you there, if you don't mind, that is."

"I would love that. Come later today, we'll be there."

Leaving her to her books and thoughts, I bid her goodbye, walked out of the room, and made my way up the spiral staircase again, leaving the secret library and Ellie behind me. As I climbed up each step, I couldn't help but think that this was far from over. As most things in the Orchard Hollow went, even death wasn't final in our little town. And as much as I wish to leave what happened to Sylvia behind, those marks on her neck irked me. Spurring me to find out the truth. What was the worst that could happen?

There was no harm in checking it out. Unless I mucked this up and made waves where there weren't any. Flashes of the crochet club flew before my eyes. Was this really a good time to be questioning the women that welcomed me so warmly? *Not everybody is a suspect*, I told myself.

I closed the door of the mausoleum behind me and stepped out into the hot air of the cemetery. I was so lost in my thoughts, I didn't even notice the broad frame of the person walking towards me. My shoulder collided with a solid chest, and I yelped, spinning around from the impact. I turned to face the poor person I had nearly run over. My eyes landed on a muscular physique, windblown hair, and a jaw that could cut glass. My chest tightened.

"Rhyven," I said in a near growl. "What are you doing here?"

"I came to see you, actually."

"Me?" I asked, flabbergasted. "How did you know I would be here?"

Rhyven raked his fingers through his hair, tousling the waves further. "I came by the manor and saw that it was locked so I figured there was only one other reasonable place to find you."

"At the cemetery?"

River nodded. "At the portal site."

The color drained from my face. My shoulders hiked up so high they touched the lobes of my ears. I looked over my shoulder at the portal site behind me then turned my attention back to the Prince of the Shadow Court. "Speaking of the portal," I said. "I've been meaning to ask you. How did you make your way to this realm?"

Rhyven crooked a bushy brow my way and looked down his nose. "That, I'm afraid, is a story for another day." He tipped his chin to the mausoleum. "How did it go in there?"

"Pardon me?"

"No need to be coy, Lyra. I know all about your little group. I'm assuming you're here to comfort your friend after what happened at the crochet club."

This time, my jaw hit the floor. I pulled it back up,

closing my gaping mouth, and asked, "And how did you know about what happened to Sylvia?"

Rhyven winked. The fool actually winked at me. "Darling, I am the Prince of the Shadow Court. There is nothing that I do not know."

"You followed me to Tangled Skeins last time, didn't you?"

He winced, holding his hands up in surrender. "You caught me."

"Oh, for the love of Fairy!" I ground out. "You need to keep a lower profile here, not be gallivanting around town. I don't know if you know this, but you stand out like a sore thumb. Half the town is already talking about you."

"All good things, I hope."

I scowled at him. "This isn't a joke. The people here, they can't know where we're from. Do you know what would happen if somebody were to find out you're a fae?"

The prince tsked. "Give me a little more credit than that, Lyra. I know how to stay hidden. You don't need to school me. I am not a child."

Then better stop acting like one.

"Besides," the prince continued, oblivious to my inner turmoil. "This town is constantly talking about someone. I'll be old news before you know it. Now, what are you going to be doing about Sylvia?"

I stopped breathing.

"I beg your pardon?" I asked.

"I thought I told you to stop playing games," Rhyven scolded. "You and I both know that was no accident. A woman that knows her way around the yarn shop doesn't fall clumsily and hit her head. Someone did this to her."

I tried to breathe, but no matter what I did, my lungs refused to expand. How did Rhyven know so much about Sylvia and the yarn shop?

"I'm not even going to ask you how you know all that," I said. "What would you suggest I do?"

"What I've seen you do many times since I got here," Rhyven said. "Investigate. Find out what the police can't. You're remarkable at it."

Heat burned my cheeks. "Oh. Thanks. But I'm sorry to disappoint you, there isn't much that I can do. Ellie already tried to talk to her Aunt Dot and she clammed up. I have the feeling the rest of the ladies will do the same. If there was any foul play in Sylvia's death, the crochet club is not going to talk about it."

There was a mischievous gleam in Rhyven's dark eyes. One corner of his lips ticked upward. He licked his bottom lip and looked at me playfully. I worked to ignore the blazing fire his gaze left behind on my skin.

"It's a good thing I'm here then," Rhyven said.

I laughed. "How do you figure? Are you a secret crochet master that I did not know about?"

"Not in the slightest," the prince replied. Then, wiggling his eyebrows, added, "But I *have* always wanted to learn. Luckily there's a crochet club in town that's short a member. Even luckier that I joined it."

Around me, the cemetery faded away. A headache careened between my temples, and I rubbed the bridge of my nose trying to subdue it. Leave it to me to find myself in yet another unbelievable scenario. There was no shaking Rhyven now, not when he was hooked deep in Orchard Hollow business.

I shook my head at the prince's self-assured smile. *Fairy help me. This was going to be some week.*

Chapter Six

I stared at Rhyven in disbelief. My eyes wide, and my mouth opening and closing like a fish out of water. "What do you mean you joined the crochet club?" I asked the Shadow Prince.

"I mean what I said, Lyra," he answered in that self-assured way. "You need inside information and what better way to get it than to be on, well, the inside."

Somewhere in the distance a car started with a loud choking sound. I looked around, forgetting for a moment that we were in the cemetery and likely shouldn't have been discussing Sylvia's death out in the open. But it was so fresh in my mind, and after the conversation I had with Ellie I couldn't help but need answers. And Rhyven wasn't wrong. It did make sense to infiltrate the club. It was the best way to get the women to open up to me. But I didn't need him to do so.

I crossed my arms and huffed out a sharp breath. "I could join the club myself," I suggested. "It would be a lot less suspicious. You don't exactly strike me. as someone who enjoys crochet. I'm sure the women wouldn't fall for it either."

Rhyven smirked. "I am the Prince of the Court of Shadows," he scolded. "Pretense and performance are a mastery of my people. You know that."

Oh, I sure do.

He didn't tell have to tell me twice. I knew exactly how deceitful the Court of Shadows and the fae that resided there could be. They were the most brutal court around and they didn't get that reputation with honesty. I had no idea how that was going to aid Rhyven here and now.

"In case you forgot, you're supposed to be keeping a low profile," I said.

Rhyven scoffed and I battled the urge to punch him in his stoic nose. "No one will know where who I am, or where I'm from," he said calmly. "I can guarantee it. Let me help you with this. Even if you *do* join the club, there is no way you're going to get anything out of the group. Especially not if the killer is amongst them."

As much as I hated to admit it, he was right again. Murderers didn't exactly go around admitting to their crimes, and they certainly didn't open up about their evil deeds to someone they had only recently met. Especially if that someone came around asking questions. And Rhyven did seem to have a way with human women ... If they didn't have a crush on him, they found him interesting. He was like a glowing light bulb in a field of moths. They couldn't help but be drawn to him.

He certainly could use that to his advantage when it came to sussing out the truth.

I opened my mouth to speak but shut it closed when the door of the mausoleum creaked open. My heart hammered in my chest as panic set in. *That must be Ellie leaving.* I had to get Rhyven out of sight before he was discovered. No matter how good the prince was at pretending to be someone else, I was not ready to explain who he was to my friends. Nor was I ready to explain what he was doing here in the cemetery. The last thing I needed was for the Wardens to think they couldn't trust me with their secret identity.

My eyes flicked from the entrance of the mausoleum to a freshly dug grave a few feet away. I rolled my eyes and sucked in a breath before shoving Rhyven backward.

"Hey!" he yelped.

With another swift shove, I drove Rhyven toward the open hole in the ground, the edge of the half-dug grave yawning like a mouth ready to swallow us both whole. The wet earth around it had begun to crumble under the weight of recent rain, making the perimeter slick and treacherous. I threw a quick glance down and felt a flicker of relief; it wasn't too deep yet. The fall wouldn't kill him. Probably wouldn't even bruise him. Not that someone like Rhyven, with all his dark magic and impossible grace, would stay bruised for long. Still, I didn't actually want to hurt him. Not right this second, anyway.

Before he could turn those dark eyes on me in protest, I planted my feet, gathered every ounce of strength I had, and delivered one final, uncompromising shove.

His balance faltered. He stumbled, his boots skidding in the loose soil as his heel caught on the uneven edge of the grave. For a heartbeat, he teetered—arms flailing slightly in an uncharacteristic moment of surprise—then gravity did the rest.

Behind me, the mausoleum door creaked violently on its hinges and slammed open, the sound reverberating through the crypt like a warning bell. I didn't stop to look. Didn't breathe. With only a flicker of hesitation, I hurled myself forward, stepping off the edge and following Rhyven down into the earth.

The world dropped out from under me. The fall was short, but sharp. My breath caught in my throat and then burst from my lungs as I landed hard on something solid and unmistakably human-shaped.

Rhyven.

His chest rose beneath me, and I could feel the flex of muscle and the faint thrum of magic that always seemed to hum just beneath his skin. The smell of wet soil closed in around us, thick and cloying. My nostrils burned from it, gritty and damp, a reminder that we were quite literally buried alive, albeit temporarily.

The space was narrow and damp, the walls pressing in on all sides, and there wasn't an inch of room between our bodies. I lay sprawled directly on top of him, my hands braced awkwardly on his shoulders, my knee jammed somewhere near his hip. Every contour of him was maddeningly present and his breath tickled my collarbone, annoyingly steady despite our undignified landing.

I shifted slightly, trying to ignore the sharp awareness flaring in my stomach. Now was not the time to be distracted by how unfairly attractive the Shadow Prince was, especially when we were hiding. I forced my attention upward, straining my ears.

Above us, the soft crunch of footsteps echoed across the cemetery grounds. Ellie.

I stilled, pressing deeper into the silence, every muscle tense and alert. Rhyven didn't move. He didn't need to. His presence alone was louder than anything he could've said.

"Not that I'm complaining," Rhyven said in a hushed tone. "Next time you need to simply ask. I would have jumped in myself, if I knew what you were thinking."

I pressed my palm to his mouth to keep him quiet. "Shh! Be quiet before she hears us," I hissed out.

Above our heads, Ellie's footsteps got lighter and lighter as she walked away from the mausoleum and put distance between her and the grave we hid in. I waited until the cemetery fell into complete silence before using Rhyven's wide chest to brace myself so I could push away from him. Slowly, I stood up and peered over the edge of the grave, my eyes scanning the cemetery for any presence of Ellie. When I was certain the coast was clear, I looked down at Rhyven and said, "Give me a boost. Let's get outta here."

To my utter shock, the prince didn't argue. Instead, he jumped up to stand, put both his hands around my waist and lifted me with such ease you'd have thought I'd weighed no more than a feather. When my feet were on solid ground again, I brushed off whatever dirt I could from my clothes—no luck, the pants would need a dry clean—and waited until Rhyven pulled himself up to stand beside me.

He watched me intently, his eyebrows drawn low

and his jaw working itself out as he considered me in deep concentration.

"What?" I barked out.

"Oh, nothing," the prince drawled. "I was thinking how beautiful you look amidst the tombstones."

There he is. That's the Rhyven I had come to expect.

I took a step backward to put some air between us and looked him up and down. "How about I make you a deal?" I asked. "I go along with your plan to infiltrate the crochet club and in return, you never use lame pickup lines on me again."

Rhyven's chest rumbled with a low laugh. "Sounds fair," he agreed, extending a hand and waiting until I shook it.

That, my friends, was how I found myself striking a deal with the Prince of the Shadow Court in a small-town cemetery standing next to a half-dug grave. Whatever warnings you may have heard about bargaining with the fae were all true. Though I knew Rhyven would likely find some way to turn this around on me, I didn't have much of a choice. If I wanted to find out what happened to Sylvia Plumwell, I had to do whatever it took. Even shake the hand of the man whose word I trusted less than that of the Grim Reaper's.

Chapter Seven

The freezing temperature in the room made the hairs on my arm stand up straight. I brushed down the crisp fabric of my work apron, snapped on a pair of latex gloves, and got to work. Before me, Sylvia Plumwell's body lay still and stoic, not a hair out of place. If it wasn't for the dried patches of blood on her pristine waves and the terrible gash to the rear of her head, I'd have thought she was sleeping.

I worked meticulously, performing a routine check as I always did when a body arrived at the funeral home. After years of performing these tasks, it was almost surreal how I could compartmentalize. Though Sylvia was very much a person that I had personally met, right now, lying on the slab in front of me with the faint sound of classical music playing in the background and the chill of the open freezer unit enveloping my skin, she was not Sylvia at all. She was a vessel that I needed to examine with the utmost care. I had learned a long time ago that to get emotional in a job like this would do more harm than good. So, I stopped being emotional and instead focused on making sure that the bodies that arrived in my morgue were prepared for their final resting place. I respected the dead as much as I respected the living. I think it was what made me good in this profession.

Now, I was doing the same thing with Sylvia Plumwell as I did with every other client to adorn my doorstep. I paused for a breath, the way I always do. Needing a moment to center myself. Then I folded the sheet further back.

Sylvia's face looked peaceful, but too perfect somehow. Makeup had been applied before she got here. That wasn't standard. Not unless the family requested a home viewing—and they hadn't. She must have come straight here from the shop.

I moved on, checking her hands. Fingernails neat except for one—middle finger, right hand. The nail was broken, jagged at the edge. Could've happened during the accident. Could've been anything else. I made a note of it in case I would need to reference it later or if the police needed to know. The wrists looked fine. No bruising. No odd marks. But right under her neck, faint and hard to spot unless you knew what to look for, there was a line. A mark. Like a necklace had been there, pressed against the skin for a long time, then taken off.

Necklaces didn't usually leave lines like that unless they're tight. And this one had a pattern to it. It was woven maybe. I didn't recognize it right away, but I knew I'd seen it before.

I took a step back, exhaled. This wasn't right. Nothing obvious, nothing you could pin down with a single photo or a report. Simply ... a feeling. A nudge in my gut I'd learned to trust. I wrote it all down—every mark, every oddity. I didn't jump to conclusions. That was not my job. My job was to pay attention. To notice what others might have missed. Sometimes the dead carried secrets in the quiet of their bodies, and sometimes, if you were patient, they whispered them to you.

When I got to the fatal wound on Sylvia's head, I had to work harder to calm myself. Bile rose in my throat and I tamped it down, focusing on examining the crack to Sylvia skull.

"How did you get yourself in this position, Sylvia?"

She didn't reply, obviously.

I grimaced, licking my lips, and pulled some of Sylvia's hair out of the way so I could take a look at the piece of evidence that truly intrigued me. Now that I was looking at Sylvia closer, the red line on her neck wasn't quite as distinct, and for a second, I thought that maybe I imagined the entire thing. Made up a scenario in my head that wasn't there because I couldn't accept the fact that she was dead. I pressed my thumb and forefinger to Sylvia's skin and stretched it slightly, leaning in closer. I narrowed my eyes. Took a good thorough look at the line. It was definitely there. Faint, but there.

What is this from? I wondered.

Carefully, I rolled Sylvia over to her side and looked at the rear of her neck, quickly realizing that the line was here as well. If she was strangled like I originally theorized, it would make sense for it to extend all the way around. But the mark was so thin, I couldn't imagine anybody's fingers being so small. A morbid thought occurred to me. *Unless they didn't use their hands.* Still, anything used to strangle somebody had to have some weight to it. I didn't know this from personal experience, but I would imagine that if Sylvia didn't die accidentally, if someone did this to her, she would have fought back. Whoever killed her must have been strong enough to restrain her long enough.

Slowly, I lowered Sylvia back down on the slab and took a step back. As I did something caught my attention at the neckline of Sylvia's blouse. I grabbed a pair of tweezers from the tray of tools on the table beside me and plucked the fiber, bringing it up to the light. It looked like a piece of string. A smooth and shiny one. The color didn't match the blouse Sylvia had on and for some reason it tugged at my attention. I walked the string over to the to the singular desk in the room and pulled over the magnifying glass attached to it. Then I inspected the string. From here it only took me a second to realize what I held in my hands.

Yarn, I thought.

Not any yarn. Judging by the fibers and the sheen of them, I'd have wagered it was silk yarn. Theories floated in my brain and I tried to grab hold of one of them as best I could. I didn't know much about yarn, but I knew enough about the general makeup of certain materials, mostly from dressing the deceased. The interesting part of silk was how strong it was. I had learned it some time ago that a strand of silk cord could be strong enough to hold up over twenty-five pounds.

My mouth flew open.

Walking back to Sylvia, I carefully positioned the strand of yarn against the red mark on her neck. The width of it fit perfectly. If I was right, and someone did strangle Sylvia in the yarn shop, here was a good chance they used silk yarn to do it.

I swallowed the acid in my mouth. This didn't prove much, at least not enough to take to Officer Brimley and get her to change her mind about this being an accident. But it was a good starting point. And it did do one thing, which was to tell me that I was on the right track. That I had to keep going.

Rhyven's face flashed before me, making my stomach turn. I knew I promised the prince the chance to prove himself by joining the club, but I couldn't trust him, and I never said I would stay out of it. Besides, now that I had this piece of silk in my hands, I couldn't very well sit down and do nothing.

I glanced at my watch. The crochet club met at three every afternoon at Tangled Skeins. If I hurried, I could make it there in time to join them. Take my shot at questioning the women and intercept Rhyven.

The prince was too flashy—I couldn't risk him getting found out or letting it slip that I was investigating the crochet club. Worse. What if he somehow outed himself and fairies?

As quickly as I could, I rolled Sylvia's body back into the freezer unit, placed the silk yarn scrap into a zip lock bag and tucked it into the drawer of my desk, then ran upstairs. I would have to drive fast to get there in time, but what was a little speeding when a possible killer was loose?

The atmosphere in the shop was a stark opposite to my first visit. It was as though Sylvia had painted the entire shop in shades of gloom and melancholy. Even the sound of the bell overhead seemed muffled as I walked in, like it, too, refused to work. Sitting in the same spot in the center of the shop was the crochet club. I looked over the group, relief flooding my body when I didn't see Rhyven anywhere in sight. Slowly, I let my gaze roll over each woman. They were busy with their hooks and their yarn and the project they held in their hands, yet no one spoke a word. Unlike the first time I visited, the women, were completely silent. There was no small talk or gossip. No pointless arguments and no teasing. It was almost as though they had completely forgotten how to speak.

I closed the door and shuffled closer to them.

Lillian, the shop owner, was no longer behind the counter and had joined the group to work on what appeared to be a baby blanket in gorgeous shades of pinks and creams and buttery yellows. Her focus peeled away from it and landed on me, her face brightening slightly. "Welcome back," she said with a tight smile.

I returned it. My gaze flicked to the empty seat between her and Edna, and I tried not to think about the fact that, had she not died, Sylvia would have sat in that same stool.

"I thought I would take you ladies up on your offer to teach me a thing or two about crochet. I hope this isn't a bad time." I stopped, wondering why I felt the need to lie to them. "Actually, I shouldn't have said that. I know this isn't the best time. I know what happened to Sylvia, and my real reason for coming here was to offer my condolences. I'm very sorry for your loss."

At my words, the women stopped working and I was met with three pairs of eyes staring at me intently.

"She came to you, didn't she?" Maggie asked.

I nodded slowly.

"And?"

I bristled. "And what?"

The librarian stabbed her hook into a bowl of yarn and set it on the table beside her. "Do you buy it? Her death, the accident. Whatever the police are saying. Do you believe Sylvia fell down, hit her head, and died from it?"

"Oh, please, Maggie!" Lillian exclaimed. "Enough with the conspiracy theories. We lost a dear friend in a terrible way; there is no need for this right now." She paused to look down into her lap. "You know, I can't help but think that if only I hadn't asked her to stay later that night, if she wasn't here helping me run the inventory, or if I had stayed behind, maybe—"

"Nothing you could have done to change it," Edna chimed in. "It is what it is. It happened. We accept it and move on."

Lillian's expression soured. She tossed the blanket she was working on to the side and brushed back her flowing hair. "Well, you'll have to excuse me if I can't get over it quite as quickly as you. Some of us cared about Sylvia deeply."

"Hey, I cared about her too!"

"Please," Maggie said with a moan. "We all know you two never got along."

Edna's brow furrowed so deeply the lines stayed red on her skin even after she relaxed. "That doesn't mean I wished for anything bad to happen to her. I'm as sad about what happened as you all are."

This is more like the club I remember from before.

I looked, from one woman to the next, unease building inside my body. If I didn't say something quickly, they might get into an argument that could tear them to pieces. All three seemed genuinely upset about what had happened to their friend and pitting them against each other was not going to help me get to the bottom of things any quicker. I brushed past the librarian's legs and sat down on the empty stool beside her, then turned to Lillian. "I didn't realize Sylvia helped you around the shop," I said, trying to change the subject.

"She has more so lately," Lillian replied. "I've had some things to take care of, things that took me out of the shop now and again. Sylvia was kind enough to step in. She's been coming to the shop for as long as I can remember. If I was honest, I should have added her to the payroll a long time ago. Besides, she mentioned she made plans with a friend later that evening, some big important meeting, so I figured I'd only keep her running behind if I was there. We tended to chatter away, the two of us."

"You hired her as an employee?" I asked.

Lillian's lips pressed together tightly as she nodded. "I sure did. Best decision I'd made in a long while. Sylvia loved this place almost as much as I did. Sometimes, I think she loved it more. And now ..." Her words trailed off as sadness overwhelmed her face. Her eyes flicked away from me, wetting.

My heart clenched to see Lillian this way. Whatever the shop owner's reason was for not being there the day Sylvia died, I could tell she held herself personally accountable for her death. I knew what guilt like that would do to a person—I remembered my own guilt over leaving my mother behind very well. I reached over to give Lillian's hand a gentle squeeze. "There was nothing you could have done. The police said she fell. It was a foolish accident, a terrible one, but an accident none-theless."

I bit down on the inside of my cheek before I said anything to show that I thought otherwise.

"I suppose you're right," Lillian said. "I can't believe she's gone."

"It is quite shocking," Maggie agreed. "Thank goodness Mortimer was there when I received the news or I don't know what I would have done."

I turned around to face her. "You were with Mortimer when you found out about Sylvia?"

"Yes," the librarian replied. "Our weekly poker game. I would have thought he told you."

"He didn't," I admitted.

Maggie scoffed, pushing her gold frames further up her nose. "Well, that's probably because he's a sore loser."

With that, I picked up a ball of yarn and a spare crochet hook from the table, letting the soft strands slip through my fingers as I feigned interest in the project. My hands moved automatically, muscle memory taking over while my mind stayed sharp, tuned to Edna's every twitch and breath. The hook felt oddly comforting in my hand—a familiar weight, anything to anchor me while I tiptoed through the conversation.

I cast on a few sloppy stitches, not caring if they amounted to anything. The point wasn't the scarf or square or whatever it might become: it was to look busy, harmless, like someone simply passing the time in a circle of small-town chatter. I glanced at Edna out of the corner of my eye, noting the way her fingers twisted in her lap, her lips pressed together too tightly.

"What about you?" I asked, keeping my voice casual

as I looped the yarn again. "Where were you when you heard about Sylvia passing?"

The woman's brows shot up high into her skull. "Me? Oh. At home."

"Alone?"

Edna's hands continued to stay busy. "Well, yes. Who else would I be with?" she asked quickly. Her gaze darted from side to side, and for a second. she looked like I had made her uncomfortable.

I glared at Edna. Trying to gauge her body language.

One might even say that she looks guilty.

In my head, I calculated the possibilities. The women did get into a heated argument about the pattern Sylvia brought up. And now Edna's alibi was shaky at best. She did seem genuinely upset with Sylvia the other day but upset enough to kill her? And in such a horrible way? I wasn't sure.

The bell rang overhead and a group of people walked in, forcing Lillian to stand up and help her new customers. As soon as she was gone, it was as though a spell was broken. The women returned to their silent crocheting. They worked so precisely, their eyes never leaving their projects. Almost as though they did not wish to speak to me any longer. No one offered to help me learn as Sylvia had and judging by the scowls on their faces, no one would. I could almost laugh, picturing Rhyven attempting to impress these women. *Good luck to you, Prince.*

Making up an excuse to leave, I waved goodbye to Lillian and rushed out of the shop. The warmth of the air outside did little to placate my chilled bones. Everything about what happened rubbed me the wrong way. One of those women was hiding something. I didn't know what and I didn't know why, but they were lying. Maybe not even one ... maybe all of them.

I pulled my phone out of my bag and dialed the number I had all but memorized by now. The line rang twice before a friendly voice picked up on the other end. "Orchard Hollow Police Station. How can I help you?"

"Hello, this is Lyra Moore. I'm the funeral director. Over on—"

"Yes, yes, I know who you are," the woman interrupted me. "Who can I get for you?"

I cleared my dry, patchy throat. "Oh, Officer Brimley," I said quickly.

There was a silence on the line, followed by the sound of keyboard keys clicking away.

"I'm afraid she's not in today," the receptionist said. "Anyone else I can get for you?"

I frowned, my head lolling back and my eyes rolling skyward. "No, I really did need to speak to Officer Brimley," I said, biting my bottom lip. "Actually, maybe you could answer a question for me. I didn't see any personal belongings brought in with Sylvia Plumwell's body. Do you happen to have anything of hers at the station?"

"Let me take a look in the system," the woman said.

There were more keys typing away as the receptionist got to work followed by a prolonged silence that drove me right out of my skin. After what seemed like a century, the line crackled as the receptionist came back on. "Miss Moore?"

"Yes, here."

"We have a purse belonging to a Sylvia Plumwell. Did the family request it?"

I cleared my throat once. Twice. "Oh, no one has been by to see her yet," I replied. "But family members usually request to have the deceased belongings. So, if someone could drop that purse by, I'd be happy to pass it on when they do."

"Sure thing, Hon. I'll have an officer pop by later this afternoon with it. Anything else?"

I coughed into my hand. "Yes, as a matter of fact, do you happen to know if there was a crochet pattern in the purse?"

"A crochet pattern?"

I chuckled. "Yes, I know it sounds foolish, but it was very important to Sylvia. I was thinking it might be nice for her family to have it."

"I don't see a crochet pattern in the inventory," the

receptionist answered. "I can go and check personally if you'd like."

"No, no. There's no need for that," I said. "Thank you for all your help."

"Anytime, Miss Moore. You have yourself a great day."

As the receptionist hung up, my eyes drifted from the bright sky to the large window of the yarn shop. Sylvia was obsessed with that pattern. There was no way she would go anywhere without it. And she did mention having it on her at the club meeting, which means that it would have been there when she died. A hole formed at the base of my stomach and a shiver tripped down my spine. The only way that pattern would be gone is if someone took it after Sylvia passed away. It was beginning to look like I was wrong after all. Crocheting was a killer hobby and Sylvia's pattern may have been worth enough to kill her for.

Chapter Eight

I stared at the roses lining the porch in disbelief. Beside me, Rhyven's bushy brows furrowed, and he nudged me with his elbow. "This is interesting," the prince said.

My knees knocked together as I took in the deep orange shade of the flower petals. Interesting was one way to put it. Absolutely terrifying was another. When I came home to find Rhyven on my doorstep, I almost didn't notice the roses that had appeared to have changed color in the short time I was gone. My attention was focused solely on the prince and figuring out why he had come to my home uninvited. Again. Now his presence was surprisingly welcome since he was the one person that knew about magic and had seen the roses shift colors before.

"Why do you think it's happening?" I asked.

Rhyven shrugged. "I wish I knew. The green fae in our realm can alter the makeup of certain flowers."

I shook my head. "I thought of that too, but even the strongest green fae need to have a strong base magic to do so. Not to mention the intention to change the flower's internal DNA. I had neither of those things. It wasn't like I chose to do this." I paused, remembering the first time the flowers changed from the blood red they'd always been to a bright purple. "And twice at that." I looked at Rhyven, concern lining my face. "Something is terribly wrong with my magic."

"Let's not jump to conclusions. It could be nothing."

"Or it could be everything."

The prince knelt next to the roses, brushing his finger along one petal. The flower shivered as though it was afraid of his touch. In his hand, the orange hue appeared even brighter, like it was on fire. I bristled. *Great.* The last thing I needed was for a garden to catch fire. Nothing quite screamed "Hey, look at me. I'm a fairy!" like color-changing roses and magical gardens. If I wanted to stay under the radar in the human realm, I needed to get a handle on whatever this was, and I needed to do it fast. A thought popped into my head and I spun on my heels to face Rhyven. "Do you think this has anything to do with the portal I opened?"

"Maybe," the prince said. "Have you tried to open it again?"

"Yes. But unfortunately, I've had no luck," I replied. "Which is another reason why I think my magic is on the outs."

Rhyven stood up, brushing dirt off his knees. "I wouldn't go so far. Portal magic is rare, and from what I gather, you're not an expert in using it. Is it safe to assume that the only reason you opened the first portal was because you were trying to escape?"

I press my lips tightly together and sucked in a breath through clenched teeth. "Well, yes, of course. But —" I paused, "—perhaps you're right. The two might not be connected."

"I never said that. The roses did change color for the first time when you opened the portal."

And the first time you *arrived in this realm,* I thought.

"I say we test it out," Rhyven continued. "Let's see if you can open a portal and what effect it will have on the flowers."

I glowered at him. "How do you propose I do that? I just told you that the first time it happened was completely by accident and that I haven't been able to open one since."

"What if I help?"

My eyes widened at the prince in disbelief. "How? You don't have portal magic."

"But I do have a magic," Rhyven countered. "I can siphon some of my magic to amplify the power you have. It might work."

"You-you would do that?" I stammered.

I must have heard wrong. There was no way Rhyven was suggesting he'd give me some of his magic. There wasn't one fae in all of Fairy that would be willing to do that for another. Not even my own mother has ever lent me her magic, and I knew she'd loved me fiercely. To give up your magic for another fairy was like giving up a part of your soul. For Rhyven to offer it so freely, especially when his magic was the type that most fae greedily yearned for, was unprecedented. The Shadow Court was the strongest court in our entire realm and the royals of that court, especially ones as powerful as Rhyven, had the most precious magic in the realm. And he was going to give some of it to me?

I rolled my shoulders back and looked at him through my lashes. "I can't ask you to do that."

"You're not asking," Rhyven said. "I'm offering. If it helps us figure out why your magic is malfunctioning, I'm more than happy to lend a hand. It's only a few shadows anyway."

I coughed. *A few shadows? Right.* More like a magical source that's strong enough to blast all of Earth into nothingness. And yet what choice did we have? As much as I didn't want to accept this profound gift from Rhyven of all people, I needed to figure out what was wrong with me before I caused something worse than a flower to change color.

Against my better judgment, I took a step towards the Shadow Prince and said, "All right. I'm in. What do we do now?"

"You tell me." Rhyven shook his head. "I know nothing about portals, so why don't you try to do what you did before, and I'll lend a hand from the sidelines?"

I looked between the prince and the roses then took a deep breath in to settle my racing mind. My thoughts were all over the place. If I had any chance of even remotely opening this portal, I had to concentrate. I closed my eyes and pictured the doorway in my head. Then I dug deeper, imagining every inch that I saw from the snow-covered land before. I thought of it until I grew frigid cold, even though it was summer. Until my bones shivered and goosebumps spread all over my arms. My hair stood on edge, lips shivering. I gritted my teeth together, rubbing my palms over my forearms to stay warm. In my mind, the land of ice took form. I imagined the same barren landscape; the same unruly winds blowing through. I imagined everything I had seen in my nightmares. When I felt as though it was right in front of me, my magic soared to the surface and covered every inch of my skin. I opened my eyes as rainbow lights surrounded me in a rushing swirl of glowing colors. Giving Rhyven one quick glance, I thrust my hands out toward the empty driveway and blasted it with my magic.

Nothing happened.

Growling, I tried again. This time Rhyven joined in. When his magic collided with mine, it was like my world turned upside down. My stomach dropped to my feet and my heart raced so fast I thought it was going to jump out of my rib cage. My pulse hammered between my ears. Rhyven spoke, but I couldn't hear him. His words were merely a mumble. I felt his magic course through me, and I wanted more, more, more. I was hungry for it. Ravenous. I yanked on that, pulling more from him until his eyes widened and his teeth split open in a gasp. Taking what I could, I threw both our magic out into the world of frost at the forefront of my mind. Near to me, Rhyven hissed as I siphoned more of his magic.

Again, the portal remained unopened.

I dropped my arms down to the side, limp. Beside me, Rhyven's shoulders dropped, and he rubbed his forehead as my grasp on his magic evaporated. We looked down at the roses in unison. A bright, fiery orange.

"That was interesting," Rhyven said.

"You really need to think of another adjective," I scolded. "It didn't work."

"It was worth a try. We'll keep at it. We'll figure it out."

My eyes narrowed on him. "How can you be so certain?"

"There has to be a logical answer to why this is happening, and even if there isn't, even if you are the first fairy to ever have this power, we'll figure it out."

"But my magic—"

"Stop," Rhyven said sternly. "There is nothing wrong with your magic. You are exactly as you're supposed to be. Your magic is different, that's all. It's quite all right to be different."

I started to argue when the sound of gravel crunching under tires made me stop in my tracks. Turning away from Rhyven, I looked at the car approaching the driveway, dread overtaking me whole. It continued to eat away at me as the car parked and Finn walked out. His posture was rigid as he approached us, and I could tell by the look on his face that he was as uncomfortable as I was. His eyes continued to flick between Rhyven and me, a questioning look overtaking his features. As he got closer that look became more pronounced, morphing into something else entirely. Something more akin to jealousy.

"Good afternoon," Finn said.

Good afternoon. That was oddly formal.

I smiled and took a shot at looking as welcoming as possible. "Hey, Finn. How are you?"

The morgue director returned my smile, but it barely reached his eyes. "I'm good. Came by to see if you wanted to grab a tea in town. If you're not too busy, that is," he said.

I didn't fail to notice that at those last words, his gaze was directly glued to the Shadow Prince. I cleared my throat. At the same time, Rhyven extended a hand saying, "Finn O'Malley I presume."

"Oh. Yes," Finn said, clearly caught off guard. "I don't believe we've met."

"We haven't," Rhyven assured him. "I'm a friend of Lyra's from back home. She's told me a lot about you."

"She has?" Finn asked.

"I have?" I joined in.

Rhyven smiled his winning politician smile. "You know, Lyra. Always so secretive. It's great to run into you, always nice to meet another of her friends."

The corners of Finn's lips dragged downward. "I didn't realize Lyra had friends in town."

I had better jump in before these two destroyed each other. My mouth twisted as I said, "Rhyven was just leaving, actually." Casting a side glance at the prince, I added, "But I am afraid that my day is fairly booked with work, so I'll have to take a rain check on that tea. I'm sorry."

A shadow crossed Finn's face, but he recovered quickly, warming his features into a smile. "That's quite all right. It was a spontaneous gesture. I'll take that rain check, though, anytime you're ready."

"Are you certain you don't need me to ..." Rhyven started to ask.

I put my hand up to cut him off. "I'm all set here. Thank you both for stopping by but I really must get back to work."

With that, I spun on my heels and marched up the steps of the porch. Clumsily unlocking the three locks of the front door of the manor, I pushed my way inside and shut the door firmly behind me. I didn't bother checking to see if the men had gone. Instead, I pressed my back to the door and slid all the way down to the floor, my butt hitting the floorboards with a dull thud. My pulse continued to rise as the last few minutes replayed in my head. Since when did life in Orchard Hollow become so unbelievably hectic? I came here to escape the absolute insanity of my homeland, but instead, found myself in the midst of more chaos.

Between the deaths and the men and the changeling cat that was now screaming my name from upstairs, I wasn't sure if I was cut out to handle this. I heard the sound of a car pulling away outside followed by retreating footsteps. Dragging my knees up, I dropped my head in between them and counted to ten. Then twenty. Then Fifty. Tremors shook my body and it took a while for me to start to feel like myself again. My hands reached for the cell phone in my back pocket. Typing rapidly, I sent a message to Ellie asking her if she wanted to meet up to discuss Sylvia's case. She replied in seconds as I knew she would. That was one thing I could count on with Ellie Blackwood—she was always up for a distraction. Especially when that distraction involved solving a possible murder.

Chapter Nine

I passed back and forth in front of the yarn shop, the to-go cup of tea in my hands splashing from side to side. My gaze rolled over the colorful balls of yarn displayed in the window, and I peered in between them to the crochet club gathered inside. All seemed the same except this time there were two members that weren't there before. One I expected to see here since she invited me to join when I suggested we meet up. The other ...

I watched Ellie haul a fresh tray of tea and scones for the club, depositing it on the side table with shaky hands. A blueberry scone rolled off the tray and fell onto the floor, crumbs flying everywhere, but my dear friend didn't even notice. Her attention was entirely rooted on the newest member of the crochet club and the second person catching me off guard today. I mumbled a few fae curse words under my breath as I watched Rhyven laugh obnoxiously at something Ellie's aunt said. His fingers moved quickly as he listened intently to the woman, an intricate crochet basket coming to life in his expert hands. Frustration grew to the size of a beach ball inside my gut. Was there anything the Prince of the Shadow Court was not good at? His eyes flashed to me and I buckled backward, startled. Noticing me outside, Rhyven smirked. I growled.

Rolling my eyes, I gripped the cup tighter and made my way into the shop. This time, no one even bothered to look up as the bell rang out over my head. Much like Ellie, they were focused on the tall, dark, and handsome prince in their midst.

Groaning audibly, I inched closer to the group then cleared my throat when I still got no response from the women. "Hello everyone," I uttered.

"Lyra. Come in, come in. Join us," Lillian exclaimed.

I noticed that she wasn't looking at me when she said it.

"Hey," Ellie remarked, finally peeling her gaze off Rhyven. "Glad you could make it." She pulled out a chair next to the prince and gestured for me to sit down. "Would you believe we got a new member?"

I cast Rhyven with a death glare.

"What a pleasant surprise," I said through gritted teeth. "It's nice to meet you."

The prince breathed in slowly, his chest widening and obscuring the back of his seat entirely. He extended a hand my way, flexing his muscles as he did. "The pleasure is all mine," he purred. "The name is Rhyven. And who might you be?"

I fought the urge to throw up on his shoes as my lunch came back up into my throat. "Lyra Moore," I said innocently.

"Are you a fellow crocheter?"

I bit the inside of my cheek before answering. "Only here for moral support." Then, nodding at the basket in his lap, I added, "You seem to be incredibly good at it."

"Oh, this small thing?" Rhyven asked. "Would you believe that this is my first time attempting it?"

Somehow, I can.

I shook my head. "Well, you have a natural talent," I told the prince. "I'm surprised I haven't seen you in the shop before."

"Oh, Rhyven is new in town," Edna cut in from her wingback chair.

"We would have remembered him if he wasn't," Dot chimed in.

I rubbed my temples. Was no one in this town safe from the prince's wiles? The last time I was here, all the ladies did was bicker uncontrollably and now, one visit from Rhyven, and what? They were the best of friends? This was unbelievable. Trying to avoid Rhyven's not-so-casual looks, I concentrated on the group to gauge their behavior. I knew that at least one of them was lying and as expected, most knew more about what happened to Sylvia than they let on. But without an in and with Rhyven and Ellie here, I couldn't very well interview the ladies. Not without throwing suspicion on myself or the true reason for my presence at the club. So, I did the next best thing. I picked up a spare crochet hook from the table, grabbed a ball of yarn and proceeded to stab at it like I knew what I was doing.

We worked for almost an hour with the women chattering on about all of the town's business to fill Rhyven in on every piece of gossip they could muster. I had to hand it to the prince, he played the part of a newcomer to Orchard Hollow quite well. Rhyven nodded and listened, laughed at all the right moments, and, as much as I didn't want to admit it, he truly was exceptionally good at this.

It never occurred to me that Rhyven might be an excellent sidekick. It wasn't until I glanced at the basket in his hands that I realized that he may have been right after all—I never should have doubted letting him infiltrate the club. Not only did he create the most intricate and gorgeous design I had ever seen, but he fit in remarkably well with the women. Much better than me, whose clumsy hands had created yet another catastrophic mess of yarn.

I grumbled under my breath with each pointless stab of my crochet hook. After a while, the conversation teetered off, being replaced by the sound of yarn being looped around hooks and the occasional clinking of a teacup. Sitting next to her aunt, Ellie clicked away on her laptop because, as I figured, she wasn't actually an active member of the club. Watching my friend get up several times to refill Dot's teacup made me realize her attitude toward her aunt was only a front and it was nice to see that Dot had someone to lean on at this awful time.

After the fourth refill, the tea had run dry and Ellie stood up to put a new pot on only to be stopped by Dot. "Sit down and relax, dear," she said. "I'll get the next round."

"But—"

Dot grabbed the teapot from Ellie's hands, silencing her instantly. "I won't hear anything of it. It's sweet of you to come and lend a hand, but I know what you're doing, young lady. And believe me when I say, I don't need a babysitter."

Ellie's cheeks turned to a bright shade of red. She let go of the tray, reluctantly allowing her aunt to take the reins. This was my way in, and I wasn't about to waste it. Brushing past Rhyven, I walked after Dot toward the rear of the shop where I assumed a small kitchen awaited. "Let me help you with that," I offered. "I could use this chance to stretch my legs a little."

With an understanding nod, she pushed open a small door behind the main counter with her hip and waited until I followed her to let it swing closed behind us. I followed Dot past a wall of boxes, each one labeled with a different name of yarn. I couldn't help but notice how much yarn there was in the place. The shelves in the shop were already quite full and taking this inventory into account, I was beginning to wonder if anyone was buying yarn at Tangled Skeins at all. From the looks of these boxes, I highly doubted it. In fact, come to think of it, with the exception of the crochet club and a few straggling customers I'd barely noticed anyone visiting the shop.

Dot swung open another door and the tight, cramped corridor opened up to a large kitchen. There was a long counter on the far side of the room, a full-size fridge, and even a dishwasher. The room was almost as big as the kitchen in the manor, which was surprising for a business establishment.

"Lillian used to live in the small apartment at the rear," Dot said, noticing me staring.

I nodded. "She doesn't anymore?"

"Not for a while, no. She rented it out last year, but the tenant moved out and there hasn't been any interest in it since. The new girl, Betty, asked about it, I believe, but I'm not sure if anything came out of it."

"Oh," I said, unsure of how to reply further.

"Honestly, I'm not sure why Lillian tried to rent it in the first place. It's not exactly a residential area."

I shrugged. "Maybe she needed the extra income."

"I would think so," Dot said.

Her brows creased deeply, and she gave me a look that implied there was more to the story than she was willing to let on at the moment. I didn't press on, choosing instead to take the tray from her hands to place on the counter. After filling the teapot from the large farmer's sink and turning on the stove, I turned around to face Ellie's aunt again. "I've been meaning to ask ... How have you been holding up?"

"As good as can be, dear," Dot said, her voice hitching higher.

"It's never easy to lose someone," I offered. "Especially not a best friend."

Dot chuckled. "I see Ellie's been talking to you."

"She's worried about you, that's all."

The woman brushed me off with a small wave. "She's a sweet girl, that one. A lot on her mind, and she can get snippy sometimes, but a sweet girl, nonetheless. I keep reassuring her there's nothing to worry about, but she won't let it drop."

"That's Ellie for you." I laughed. "Always pressing."

Then, pausing for a moment, I said, "Something's been on my mind lately about Sylvia."

At my words, Dots eyes widened, and her ears perked up. "What about Sylvia?"

"I was thinking about the pattern that she found. The one that Edna seemed so upset about. Do you think it's true about it belonging to Edna's great-grandmother?"

"Oh, stop now. Those two were always at each other's throats. Sylvia would never take anything that didn't belong to her. She wasn't a thief. No matter what Edna seems to think. Besides, Sylvia was convinced that the pattern was written by Alaric Vionnet and, last I checked, Edna wasn't related to any fancy schmancy fashion designers long passed. And I'll tell you what. Whatever secret that pattern may have held, it doesn't matter. All Sylvia wanted was to use it. Make good use of it."

I swallowed. "She *did* make it sound like there was a pretty big secret buried in the pattern."

"Yes, well, that was just the way she was, is all. Always blowing things out of proportion. Trust me, if that pattern was worth anything, it wouldn't be Edna who'd be after it. It'd be Lillian."

I stopped short, the breath rushing from my lips. "Why Lillian?"

"Because of the Brighton Glass business, of course.

Wouldn't you want to discover some big treasure worth a whole ton of cash at the same moment that your shop was going under? I'd bet you that if there was any money to be had from that pattern, Lillian could sure use it to get Mr. Glass off her back."

Behind me, the kettle screamed as it boiled over, spurring Dot into action. She pushed past me, turned off the stove, placed the kettle back on the tray, and started for the exit. As she reached the door, she looked over her shoulder at me, asking, "Are you coming?"

I made my way after her reluctantly. The entire walk down the corridor of boxes and back to the shop I replayed her words in my head. Dot was certainly onto something. If what Sylvia thought about the pattern was true and it did hold a secret that could be worth a pretty penny, then it wasn't the strangest idea that somebody might want to cash in on it. Someone, perhaps, that had a lot on the line worth saving. I stepped out into the yarn shop and looked directly at Lillian. Maybe Sylvia's good friend was not so innocent after all.

Chapter Ten

I sat on the front porch of Mistbrook Manor with my feet dangling from the wooden bench. Across from me, perched on the railing, Theo bathed in the sunshine, his gray fur rippling every time he stretched further on the wooden beam. No matter what the changeling said about being stuck in the human realm, the place sure agreed with him. I somehow doubted Theo would have quite such a leisurely existence back in Fairy. Changelings were considered to be akin to nomads back home—they never stayed in one place very long. Although that could have been attributed to how often they swapped their children for human ones. The entire concept of placing changelings in human homes was archaic, and for the most part, the majority of changeling families didn't follow in the practice. But there remained settlements of changelings that believed in the old ways and refused to stray far from the rules. For some reason, I had the inkling that Theo had come from such a settlement. It would explain why he was so eager to leave Fairy behind despite how often he complained about doing so.

"Any answer yet?" the cat asked in between paw licks.

I tapped the refresh button on my e-mail, shaking my head. "Nothing so far," I replied.

"Don't worry," Theo said. "He'll come around."

The him that Theo was referring to was none other than Brighton Glass, a tech tycoon who was fairly easy to track down. After my conversation with Dot at the shop, I decided to take matters into my own hands and reach out to Mr. Glass to see if there was any truth to Dot's accusations. With little effort, I found the website for his tech company online which conveniently had a contact e-mail. Before my cowardly heart had a chance to say no, I sent a quick, straightforward message to Mr. Glass asking him about his interest in Tangled Skeins. I had mentioned that I was a friend of Lillian's and was concerned that she was making the wrong business move. In short, I was as honest as I could be, save for accusing Brighton Glass of threatening to take Lillian's shop away.

A part of me was convinced that I would never hear

back from him, but another part of me somehow knew better. People were fairly predictable, and from my experience, when you accused someone of anything close to the truth, they had an intrinsic need to defend themselves. I was counting on Brighton to do exactly that.

Stretching my legs out in front of me, I rearranged the laptop on the bench and opened a new search tab. Casting a quick glance at Theo, I cracked my knuckles and typed in a new query. There was no point of waiting for pixie dust to settle while I waited for Mr. Glass to reply. So, I may as well make myself useful. Instead of sitting around and twiddling my thumbs, I decided to see what I could uncover about the crochet pattern Sylvia found. My first thought was to research the pattern itself but after several tries, I came up almost completely empty. Except for a small mention in an obscure blog that hadn't been updated in years, the pattern was basically nonexistent. *Making it all the more valuable,* I thought.

I was close to giving up when I realized there was another avenue I could take in my search. Dot mentioned that Sylvia believed the pattern was written by Alaric Vionnet. Maybe, if I looked into the designer I could find something interesting.

Typing quickly, I input the designer's name into the search bar and clicked enter. *Bingo!* Whoever Alaric

Vionnet was, he sure was popular. I opened tab after tab, each one detailing information on the designer. There were articles about his work, his personal history, even one article that listed all the jobs he had before he became a famous fashion designer. And to think someone this well-known lived right here in Orchard Hollow. What were the chances? Most celebrities had moved out to King City or some other place where it would be easier for them to live out more frivolous lives, but not Alaric. He seemed to be very happy to stay right here in town. It was quite lovely when you thought about it.

I clicked on an image and enlarged it, studying the man more intently. "This guy was certainly an eccentric," I told Theo.

The cat looked up at me. "What guy?"

"The designer. The one that Dot said created the pattern."

"Could you question him about it?"

"Afraid not," I replied. "Alaric Vionnet has been dead for quite some time. Most of his work can now be found in museums. It appears that his fashion house died away with him. He had no children to inherit the business."

Theo perked up his furry ears. "Maybe that's why the pattern is worth money."

"Hmm," I mused. "It's possible. I wonder if there's a way to check how much it would be sold for now."

Typing in the designer's name and the word crochet pattern into another search bar, I pulled up several listings at auction houses in the city. I turned the screen toward Theo with a disappointed scowl. "Looks like they're not worth a lot. At least not the ones listed in these auction houses."

As I scrolled down the search results, an article published decades ago caught my attention. I clicked on the link, reading over as my eyes widened with every word. My breath felt like it had been knocked out of me. I looked up from the article and stared at Theo, slack jawed. "You're not going to believe this."

Theo looked at me like he had no interest in what I had to show him. Ignoring the cat's rude attitude, I rolled my eyes and scrolled back up on the article to read. "It appears Alaric Vionnet had a press conference not long before he died."

"Why would that be unbelievable?" Theo finally asked.

I grinned. "Because according to this, he held the conference to tell the public about a new pattern, he was going to release. A crochet pattern. Apparently that would have been enough to get the press in a tizzy since Alaric was mostly known for his knitwear collections.

But that wasn't what made this pattern so incredible," I whispered.

"For a fairy's nose, Lyra! Will you spit it out already?" Theo yelped. "What could make it such a magical piece? Isn't it yarn and a hook?"

I tsked at him. "Not this one. Alaric said that this pattern will be the only copy to be released and that in it he hid a very precious secret." I looked at the cat narrowly. "The pattern was supposed to lead one lucky person Alaric Vionnet's entire fortune."

The cat stopped mid-lick, lowering his paw to finally give me his full attention. "You don't say."

"I don't," I replied. "But this article does. I wonder if this was what Sylvia was referring to which she said the pattern was special?"

"What else could it be?" the changeling asked.

Before I could reply, my laptop dinged, making me jump in my seat. An e-mail had come in. Peeling my attention away from the article, I opened my e-mail, my legs shaking with excitement when I saw Brighton Glass's name pop up in my inbox. "It's him," I screeched. "He wrote back!"

I opened the e-mail, scanning it once, then twice, then a third time. Nerves clutched at my body with each new word read.

"What did he say?"

I glanced at Theo. "Well," I started. "He was after

Lillian's shop, after all. Wanted to turn it into some tech base for his upcoming start-up. But he says that Lillian was adamant about not selling. He even threw a ton of cash at her."

"And she didn't take it? Bizarre."

"Brighton says that Lillian told him she didn't need his money. That she and her shop were going to be fine."

The cat tipped his chin in my direction. "Fine because she might have stumbled upon a fortune from a certain fashion designer?"

My shoulders hyped up.

"What did this Mr. Glass say about your accusations of extortion? A heavy-handed approach if you ask me."

I stuck my tongue out at the cat. Sure, he had a bit of a point I supposed—I didn't need to end my letter by asking Brighton if he was threatening Lillian to get to her shop and by reminding him that extortion was not how one got what he wanted. But I truly couldn't help myself. The thought of this big-shot tech entrepreneur taking advantage of a sweet woman running a small business made my blood boil. I could only imagine how I would feel if I was in Lillian's shoes.

Angry, probably.

Across from me, Theo raised a questioning furry brow. I frowned, reading over the last paragraph of Brighton's e-mail. "He said that he did no such thing.

And that he would sue me if I continued to slander his name."

Lillian's smiling face flashed in my mind as I re-read Brighton's e-mail. I shivered, thinking of the shop owner. She may have been sweet with anyone who visited Tangled Skeins, but I was starting to think otherwise. There was a very good chance that Lillian Everwood killed Sylvia for the pattern and the fortune it contained. And if that was the case, I was going to prove it.

Chapter Eleven

The rest of my afternoon was spent hanging about town and wasting as much time as possible. Every short while or so, I made it a point to casually pass by Tangled Skeins to peer through the window. The crochet club was spending an awful long time at the shop today. On any other day. I wouldn't have minded, but today, I continuously checked my watch, my heart pitter-pattering in my rib cage as nerves and anxiety took over the real estate there. I needed to speak to Lillian on her own without the prying eyes and ears of the others. After the e-mail I received from Brighton, I couldn't shake the feeling that Lillian was more involved in Sylvia's death than she was letting on.

Where did this sudden large amount of money come

from? I tried not to dwell on the fact that I very much suspected her of Sylvia's murder. Even more so than I did before. My knees knocked as I stood across the street, pretending to read a book I picked up a few minutes earlier from a local shop. If anybody were to ask, I wouldn't be able to tell them the title of said book let alone what the first paragraph was, which was what I pretended to read over and over again as I watched the shop doors with the intensity of a trained eagle. When they finally flew open and a horde of women poured out, crochet hooks and yarn in hands, I nearly dropped the book on the ground. My clammy fingers wrapped around the spine and I flipped another page, my eyes darting between the book and Lillian's shop.

It didn't take long for everyone to exit the store. The crochet club was followed by a several customers holding paper bags with the shop's logo stamped on them. The door swung closed behind them loud enough to echo down the street. I waited for another ten minutes before all the lights turned off inside Tangled Skeins and Lillian stepped out. She locked the front door of the shop, double checked the knob several times, then took off speedily down the street. Her eyes flicked from side to side as she walked in a paranoid manner. Occasionally she glanced over her shoulder, as though she knew I was following her. *If only I had illusion magic,* I thought. *It sure would have come in handy right about now.* Unfortunately, the only magic I possessed was the green kind and it wasn't as though I could wrap myself in a floral bouquet to stay hidden.

I darted into a shadowed entranceway to watch the shop owner cross the street. Her neck twisted a few more times as she checked on her surroundings before stepping into another establishment. I rolled my gaze up to the sign above the door.

Kale Me Crazy.

It appeared that Lillian was making a stop for an early dinner before heading home. Rolling my shoulders, I ran across the street, opened the door of the restaurant, and stepped inside. I was immediately greeted by the warm scent of turmeric, roasted garlic, and something green that made me feel healthier simply by breathing it in. The place was a riot of color and texture, like a Pinterest board come to life.

Planters hung from the ceiling in mismatched macramé slings, their trailing spider plants adding to the jungle vibe of the restaurant.

Light streamed in through oversized front windows, bouncing off white tile and reclaimed wood. The tables didn't match at all. One was a vintage sewing machine base with a butcher block top, another looked like it had been salvaged from an old school science lab, burn marks and all. But somehow, it worked. It felt intentional. Artsy. A chalkboard menu behind the counter listed smoothie names like "Spirulina Sunrise" and "Beet It," written in swooping, cheerful script. A neon sign on the far wall declared "Don't Kale My Vibe," glowing hot pink against a backdrop of artificial wood.

I found myself smiling. It was ridiculous and clever and exactly the kind of place where you could eat a grain bowl and pretend your life was totally together.

It was also entirely not where I pictured Lillian Everwood spending her evenings.

The restaurant was surprisingly busy for the time of day. There were only two open tables left after Lillian had taken the one in the far-right corner. The remaining empty table was situated directly across from her but luckily the last of the three was tucked away further in the back, giving me ample space to stay out of sight.

I rushed to take my seat before I got caught, using a large menu board to hide my face as best as possible. As I read off the menu items, my stomach grumbled, and I realized that it had been some time since I ate today. Most of the things listed on the menu were outside of the scope of my regular diet, but at this point I was so hungry I could eat the board itself.

A young, bubbly server approached Lillian to take her order, quickly jotting it down on a small pad he had held in his hands before turning his attention to me. I briskly darted behind the menu again in case Lillian followed his sightline, but she was too enthralled with her phone to pay me any attention. When the server approached, I made haste placing my order—the cauliflower pizza—and returned to watching the shop owner. After several minutes of scrolling on her phone, Lillian reached into her purse to pull out a small notebook. She scribbled in it enthusiastically, put the pen down, looked at her phone again, then took more notes. Lillian was so entranced by whatever she was researching, she never once looked up to scan the restaurant around her.

What could have had her so interested?

My stomach grumbled again and the couple one table over glanced at me. I smiled sheepishly at them and gulped down the ice water the server left behind in hopes of making my hunger subside. It didn't.

Peeling my gaze off the couple, I turned back to Lillian to find her in the same position as before; scribbling in that notebook. She must have been writing for a good twenty minutes because both our orders had arrived, and while I scarfed mine down without so much as swallowing, Lillian's meal remained untouched. After some more writing, she finally put her pen down, ate half of her sandwich, then pushed way from the table. At first I thought she was leaving, but she didn't head for the front door nor take her things with her. Instead, she scooted around the few tables that lined the far wall to make her way to the rear of the restaurant where I assumed the bathrooms were located.

My brain caught fire as my gaze landed on her unattended notebook.

I should leave it alone, I told myself.

Not only should I leave her things alone, but I should pay my bill and escape from the restaurant as soon as possible. This was wrong. I was crossing so many lines I couldn't count them all in my head without needing an abacus. Since when did I start stalking people? This wasn't like me. I mean, sure, I had done a few things that were not exactly by the books to solve a case before, but I had no real proof that Lillian was up to no good, and I certainly had no proof that she was Sylvia's killer. As far as the world was concerned, I was stalking an innocent woman.

My eyes laser focused on the notebook. And yet ...

Checking the bathrooms to make sure the coast was clear, I grabbed my bag and walked straight for Lillian's table. I was so determined to get to it that it must have appeared to everybody else in the restaurant that I had every right to be there. A couple of people looked up at me as I passed, but they quickly returned to their food, paying me no mind. After one more check for Lillian and our server, both of whom were nowhere in sight, I leaped for the shop owner's notebook. As inconspicuously as I could manage, I flipped the pages trying to memorize every word I read. I was moving so fast that the words were nothing but a blur. And with my pulse thundering between my ears, it was nearly impossible to concentrate. Not to mention Lillian's handwriting wasn't exactly the neatest that I'd ever seen. I tried to make out a few of the passages, but they didn't make much sense without reading the rest of the notebook. I certainly didn't have the time for that. There were several mentions of a case but, other than that, I truly had no idea what Lillian was working on.

A slight commotion at the front of the restaurant made me teeter backward. I shut the notebook with a thud and hurried toward my own table. After leaving more than enough money to cover my meal and the tip, I dashed through the restaurant and out the door, continuing to run down the street like a complete maniac. My legs pumped and blood rushed through my veins, heating with every hurried step. Cold sweat licked the back of my neck and I swatted it away, only slowing my stride when I reached the corner and was finally out of sight of the restaurant. I bent over to place my hands on my thighs and took a few steadying breaths. This was a waste of time. Not only had I not gotten whatever it was I was looking for, but I felt quite low about what I had done. If Finn was here, or any of the Wardens, he'd tell me that we did what we needed to do to get to the truth. Yet this felt wrong to me.

I shoved all thoughts of Lillian out of my head.

It was better to let all this go and concentrate on the things that I did know about Sylvia's death. There was the pattern, the argument with Edna, and the late-night meeting Lillian mentioned in the shop. Those were the things that I knew for certain, and it was where I had to start my investigation. No more pulling at loose yarn. If I was going to find out what happened to Sylvia, I had to be strategic about it. Much like a granny square blanket, I needed to work this case one square at a time.

Chapter Twelve

The evening sun set on the horizon, painting the streets of Orchard Hollow in shades of orange, pink, and red. The colors reminded me of the roses at the Manor, which in turn reminded me of the colors they had randomly changed to, and that reminded me of my haywire magic, which then ... You get the drift.

I walked aimlessly down the steadily emptying streets, my mind racing as the surrounding shops closed their doors and people rushed into their cars, eager to leave the workday behind. It wasn't yet the peak of the tourist season in town, but the streets were already littered with people snapping photos and walking around with maps pulled up on their phones. Some even held brochures they had gotten from the local hotel as they stalked their way through the cobblestone streets, hurrying to make it to certain shops before they closed. As always, I kept to myself, frequenting the less busy passageways. In my head, I replayed everything I had learned about Sylvia's death thus far, yet no matter how I spun it, it all amounted to the same thing. A whole bunch of nothing. I wasn't any closer to finding out what happened to the crochet club member than I was days ago, and it was driving me up the wall.

Maybe it really was an accident.

I shook my head vigorously. For some reason I refused to believe it despite all the concrete evidence pointing otherwise. I wondered what had me so convinced that Sylvia didn't die by accident and that someone did actually want her dead. It must have been all the business with the crochet pattern and the so-called fortune it pointed to. Or that everyone around Sylvia was acting skittish—like they were holding back. No matter what the reason was, at some point I would have to admit to myself that I was running out of leads. Lillian was my best bet and even she appeared to be entirely innocent.

I took a sharp right at the next street corner, my head spinning. I wasn't sure how it happened, but some-how, I had ended up on the street that Tangled Skeins stood on. Even my aimless wandering brought me back to the yarn shop. It was as though my body couldn't leave what happened to Sylvia alone. I crossed my arms, suddenly feeling chilly despite the rising temperature of the encroaching summer. I truly needed to leave well enough alone. I had no time to be gallivanting around town, chasing empty leads. Not when I had a funeral home to run, a changeling cat to ignore, and two men that shall not be mentioned to avoid. My eyes caught on the flickering light inside the closed shop. I stood stock still. My breath caught in my lungs and my stomach dropped. I saw Lillian leave for the day earlier, so why was there a light on in the shop?

There shouldn't be anyone in there at this hour. My gut pulled at me to cross the street. I looked left and right, seeing that the street was entirely abandoned before dashing towards the shop. The same light I saw from before was there, faint and emanating from the back room Dot showed me on my last visit. Didn't she say there was an apartment on the premises? Maybe that's what I was seeing. Lillian's new tenant in their home. It was a plausible enough explanation, and yet I couldn't stop myself from thinking things were amiss.

My hand reached for the door handle and I twisted it, finding it locked. Eyes darting around the building, I checked for another way in. Spotting a narrow alleyway around the side I darted in its direction. A blinding darkness enveloped me as I stepped into the narrow passageway. There was not one light here to shine the way, and I had trouble seeing a foot ahead. If I was renting an apartment from Lillian, the first thing I would have done would be to ask her to install security lights back here. The place was straight out of a horror movie. I trailed my hand along the rough brick wall and felt my way down the alley, focusing on every step so I didn't accidentally trip and break my neck while I was back here. No one knew where I was. If anything were to happen, it would be days before somebody found me. If not weeks. Step by shaky step, I inched down the cramped space until finally a faint light emerged from the distance. I followed it with renewed hope blossoming in my heart. Ahead, the alley opened up to a large open space and I could finally see where I was standing. It appeared that there was a back area between one street and the next, between the buildings that stood on either side. The space was as wide as it was long. A big concrete square with nothing besides a few garbage cans lining one of the walls. There was a small lamp hanging in the corner, and it swung from side to side as a light wind rushed through. The yellow glow would normally be a welcome sight, but here, now, in this open prison chamber, it was eerie and brought a chill to my bones that I couldn't shake. To my left, I saw a door with an iron gate guarding it—the back entrance to the shop, I presumed. Carefully, I inched towards it, trying the handle and finding it locked again.

It wasn't until I spun around that I noticed the second door emerge. A small wooden thing painted in a shade of red that looked like it had seen better years. My gaze zipped from the door to the mailbox nailed in its center. *The rental unit,* I thought. My teeth clenched as I steadily approached the door. Each step closer made sweat roll into my light sweater. The light bulb swung again behind me and a terrifying pattern of shadows danced across the doorway.

I stopped breathing altogether. The door was slightly ajar.

Gulping audibly, I wiped my clammy palms on my jeans and blinked at the door. Even if there was somebody renting the unit, why would they leave that door open? Especially this late at night?

Clenching my jaw, I dared to push the door open and step inside.

The small apartment was almost the same size as the tiny outdoor space I had left behind. There was no hallway, as one would expect, the door opening directly into a cramped, dark living room. A tattered couch sat on one side of the room with a matching recliner squeezed in beside it. Before them, a coffee table stained from years of use lay oddly on one side. The seating area faced a blank wall with the outline of a picture frame long gone shaded on sage green paint. For all intents and purposes, this place did not look like it had been used in the recent years. I doubted Lillian was renting it out in such a state unless she was going to fix it up first.

I walked past the couch, ignoring the musty scent in the room, and headed into the adjoining area separated only by a makeshift half wall.

The kitchen, much like the living room, left a lot to be desired. It had all the basic necessities but none of the frills. Several of the cupboards were missing their doors like they had been pulled directly from the hinges, another indication that the apartment was not yet rentable. A sudden discomfort filled my body. I looked around the room, searching for the light I saw while standing on the street. I couldn't wait to get out of here. The place gave me the heebie-jeebies. It was a bit like being in the Winter Court in Fairy where you knew danger was lurking around every corner but there was no telling when it would jump out.

I spotted the light emerging from the end of a corridor not far from me, shooting off from the kitchen. "That must be where the bedroom is," I whispered to myself.

Following the light, I walked down the length of the corridor until I reached another opening, this one with stairs leading down. The light definitely came from below; I could see it much brighter here. My gaze darted from the staircase to the doorway across from it.

The entrance to Tangled Skeins, it appeared.

To be safe, I walked toward it and tried the lock, finding it shut. Then, spinning on my heels, I marched back toward the staircase and took a tentative step down. It was impossible to tell if anybody was down there from this vantage point, not unless I ventured all the way down. Against my better judgment, I made my way into the basement of Lillian's rental apartment.

The bottom of the stairs hit a dead end then turned to the left. As expected, this was where Lillian housed the bedroom of the apartment and much like the upstairs, it was no five-star hotel. Most of the room was obscured in shadows, but I could make out the shape of a bed and a small desk with a laptop atop it. Other than that, it was hard to tell one object from the next as I maneuvered around toward the desk. I opened the laptop screen, seeing a picture of Lillian and Sylvia pop up in the background. *This must be Lillian's computer.*

I wondered if she often used the basement to work in when she wasn't in the shop. It wasn't exactly welcoming, but who was I to judge what others did for comfort? My finger hovered above the internet icon and I pressed it, pulling up Lillian's last search. As I leaned closer to the screen, I realized she was on an adoption agency website. Was Lillian looking to adopt? I hadn't heard her or anyone else mention it.

After scrolling through the website and not finding anything of use, I closed the laptop, then, thinking twice of it, opened it again and turned off the internet browser to return everything to how I found it.

I should get out of here.

I didn't want Lillian to find me down here, and I certainly didn't want her seeing me snoop through her things. Not when I had discovered that personal information about the shop owner. Padding away from the desk, I skirted around it to make my way back to the staircase. My feet caught on an object on the ground, and I teetered forward, using the side of the desk to break my fall. I looked down to check what made me trip and surprise caught in my throat when I realized it was a cell phone. *Who would leave their phone behind?* I wondered. Bending down, I picked up the cellphone and looked at the screen, seeing the same image of Sylvia and Lillian on it. Things really weren't adding up anymore. If both Lillian's phone and laptop were here, where was she? I looked at the phone again. Blood rushed cold in my veins as I noticed the phone number pulled up on the screen, undialed. Before leaving her phone, Lillian tried to call the police. My thoughts clouded, my brain grew foggy, and dots swarmed my vision. Something was definitely wrong here.

I decided to put the phone back where I found it so as not to interfere with any possible police investigation that might follow since it had become obvious I needed to get them involved. As I bent down again, the light from the screen illuminated more off the floor; my eyes narrowed then widened so much that they nearly fell out of their sockets. Acid flooded my throat, and I had to breathe through my nose to keep the bile from suffocating me. My body shook, my legs suddenly liquid. I braced myself against the desk as I looked at the horror before me.

I completely missed seeing her before.

The way that she lay tucked behind the desk made her almost entirely hidden from sight.

"Lillian," I whispered, as I looked at the shop owner's body on the ground. "Lillian!"

Crawling towards her, I checked for a pulse but there was no use—I could already tell that I wouldn't find one. Putting her hand down, I glanced at where Lillian lay, then back towards the staircase. Her leg bent at an odd angle which told me that she must have fallen down and crawled to her phone to call for help.

She must have passed away before she got someone on the line.

My gaze caught on a broken nail in an otherwise freshly polished set of manicured fingers. *Lillian must have tried to break her fall when she slipped down the stairs,* I thought. My heart sank. There was only one thing on my mind as I pulled out my own phone to call the police. This was going to devastate Aunt Dot.

Chapter Thirteen

By the time the police got done with Lillian and the crime scene it was almost midnight and I was exhausted beyond belief. My head pounded as though somebody beat me with a hammer and, every once in a while, my body shook uncontrollably in warning that if I did not sleep soon, I would surely pay for it later. And still, even when I got home and finally laid my head on the pillow, my eyes refused to shut. Questions ran through my mind as I thought about Tangled Skeins and all the deaths that occurred there lately. Too many accidents to count. My brain itched for an explanation. How many of them were accidents at all?

I tossed and turned beneath the sheets, the fabric tangling around my legs like a net. Each twist only made it worse, the blanket wrapping tighter until the frustration bubbled up in my chest. With a sharp huff, I kicked the bedclothes off entirely, the sudden cool air brushing against my skin like a slap. The silence of the hallway was broken only by Theo's snores echoing from the room across the way—normally a familiar, grounding sound in the vast, creaky manor. But tonight, even that failed to soothe me. The snoring seemed distant, hollow, like it came from another world.

Outside, a summer storm howled with relentless fury. Rain lashed against the windows in sheets, and the wind moaned through the eaves like a grieving specter. Tree branches clawed at the glass with skeletal fingers, their scrapes and thuds like impatient knocks from something that didn't belong. The whole world felt restless: twitching, unsettled, on edge.

I let out a groan and flopped onto my back, staring at the shadow-painted ceiling. Another surge of unease crawled beneath my skin, impossible to shake. My body ached for stillness, but my thoughts refused to settle. Even the weather mirrored the churning in my chest, as if the storm had crept inside and made a home of me.

Grabbing my robe from the chair beside the bed, I put it on and headed downstairs. A nice cup of tea always seemed to do the trick when I was in one of these moods and I was hoping tonight was no different.

The stairs swam before me as my feet padded softly

on the hardwood floors, making my way to the kitchen as quietly as possible so I didn't wake the changeling. I put on a pot of tea to boil the minute I reached the kitchen. As I waited for the kettle to work its magic, I stared blankly out the small window above the sink, my eyes not focusing on anything in particular.

Suddenly, a flash of movement outside caught my attention. I jumped with a yelp then narrowed my eyes to see into the darkness, but I couldn't make anything out except the shadows that crept alongside the rose bushes. *Hmm.* I was sure I saw something. Gooseflesh tickled the back of my neck. I opened the kitchen drawer and pulled out the flashlight I kept for emergencies. Call me old fashioned, but I couldn't get used to using my phone for these things. There was something comforting about holding a flashlight when you thought someone was about to break in to murder you that really did wonders for the soul.

I was about to leave the kitchen to inspect the front yard when I stopped short, turned towards the knife block on the counter, and picked out one of the larger steak knives of the set. Then I walked to the front door. One by one, I unlatched the locks, straightened my spine, and stepped outside.

To stay on the safe side and before I ventured any further, I dug deep inside to pull on the familiar rainbow energy of fairy magic. Not far from me, the vines in the rose bushes slithered as they responded to my magic. If I was in trouble, they would help me. I wasn't sure how exactly, but I could probably use them to tie up the intruder if it came down to a fight. Fingers curling around the knife to grip the handle tighter, I pointed the flashlight towards the side of the house where I'd seen the movement before. The light from the kitchen window illuminated a lot of the space and as I stepped out, my robe floating behind me, I found I almost didn't need the flashlight at all. Shivers spread through my body and enveloped my skin with each step. I pushed away any fear I may have had and moved forward.

"Lyra," a deep voice sounded behind me.

My heart leapt into my throat. Spinning around with a gasp, I pointed the knife at my intruder and shone the light in his face. My arms lowered slightly in an instant.

"Finn?" I asked, looking at the morgue director standing at the bottom of the steps of my front porch. I shook my head, wavy hair flying everywhere. "What are you doing here at this hour?"

Finn rubbed the back of his neck. "My brother-in-law told me what happened with Lillian," he explained. "I thought you might be upset and wanted to check on you, but when I arrived, I realized just how late it was. I didn't want to interrupt in case you were sleeping. I was about to leave when you came out."

That's right, I almost forgot that Finn's late wife had a brother on the force. Word sure traveled fast in a small town, especially with two deaths so close together and under such suspicious circumstances. Though, the cops assured me that, much like Sylvia, what happened to Lillian was an accident. I tried not to laugh in their faces when they said it. How many accidents could one shop have? At this point, somebody should babyproof Tangled Skeins since, according to the police, it was less safe than an unattended construction.

Looking at Finn standing under the light of the moon all the safety I hadn't felt in a long time encompassed me. Somehow, Finn O'Malley that made me feel absolutely at home even though I was nowhere near Fairy. Did he know every little detail of my life? Absolutely not. But did it seem like he wouldn't run for the hills if I let him in? Almost certainly. It was the closest I had gotten to a true friendship since I stepped through the portal and I didn't want to lose it, even if I wasn't sure what was going to happen between us romantically anymore.

"You know, come to think of it," I told the morgue director. "I would love some company right about now. If you don't have anywhere else to be that is."

"At this hour," Finn said, "I've got all the time in the world. But maybe lose the knife."

I laughed. I waited for Finn to step into the manor

before locking the door behind us. Nudging my chin toward the kitchen and the tea kettle that was screaming to get pulled off the burner, I said, "I was making a pot of tea before you stopped by. Care to have one with me?"

"I'd never say no to a cup of tea."

It was funny, when I first met the morgue director, he was a coffee drinker through and through. It was a small detail, but somehow, I felt justified in having been able to turn him around, as if I had done the world a great deal of good by introducing Finn O'Malley to a well steeped Earl Grey. I didn't dare admit to myself that it was likely the fact that I now had an excuse to invite him over for a cup here and there that made the entire thing so much more enjoyable.

Finn settled into one of the chairs at the kitchen table and rested his elbows on the deep mahogany wood. His dark eyes watched me intently as I poured out two cups and brought them over. They rattled when I set them down and I worked not to think about the reason for my apparent awkwardness, knowing full well that it was my close proximity to Finn that was the likely culprit. Instead, I filled a small creamer with milk and set the bowl of sugar on the table between us. We sat in silence for a long time, and it was the most comfortable quiet I felt inside the manor since the time Theo decided to make a spectacle of himself and move out for the week. He didn't actually move out, of course. I caught him hiding out in the attic less than a day later, but until I found that darn cat, the quiet was almost as wonderful as the one I felt right now. Finn didn't press me for information. He didn't ask how I was. I think we both knew I wasn't doing great, all things considering. He didn't even ask me about the case, which is what I would expect from Mortimer or Ellie or Rosemary. He simply drank tea and waited until I was ready to talk. I could have stayed that way forever, but at some point, I really had to make conversation with the man. I opened my mouth to speak, but a yawn escaped me in place of words.

Finn laughed. "Do you want me to leave so you can get some rest?"

I shook my head. "To be honest, I don't think I could sleep whether you were here or not. The whole business with Lillian really has me shaken."

"I could imagine," Finn said. "Who knew crocheting was so dangerous?"

I shrugged, taking another sip of my tea. "I don't know," I murmured. "There's more to both of these deaths than meets the eye. I'm certain of it. And I know that crochet pattern is somehow connected, but I don't see who would want these two lovely women dead. Did you know Lillian was going to adopt?"

Finn shook his head.

"Well, she was. I don't know much about killers, but if she was responsible for Sylvia's death, as I suspected originally, why be looking into adoption at all? I don't know many killers who are big on family life."

"That is a good point," Finn agreed. "Maybe she was looking into it for a friend."

I rolled my tongue along my teeth. "Possibly," I said.

Noticing that Finn's cup was almost entirely empty, I reached for the pot, frowning.

"What's wrong?" Finn asked.

"We drank it dry," I answered. "Where does the time fly? Let me put another pot on. That is, if you're staying."

I was met with a raised brow. "I'm definitely staying."

The heat in his gaze made my stomach flutter with excitement. I was as giddy as a school fairy and no matter how hard I worked to calm down, the eagerness wouldn't go away. Finn often had that effect on me. As much as I hated to admit it, it would be hard to get my mind off him.

I walked over to the sink, filled the kettle, and was about to turn the stove on when I noticed an object on the counter that I hadn't seen before. A small envelope. One the size of a birthday card. There was no stamp and no address—the only thing on the front of the envelope was my printed name. Lyra Moore. I swallowed the knot in my throat, clutching the envelope tightly in my fingers and forgetting all about the tea. Peeling it open, I reached inside to pull out the contents of the envelope. Two small papers fluttered out on the counter before. Every bone in my body screamed an alarm as I looked over the first page.

"*Stay out of it,*" was all the letter read.

My tongue swelled in my mouth and my throat closed up. I put the note down, picking up the second object inside. A photograph this time.

My breath shook and my lungs worked to expand when I realized what the picture showed. It was blurry and somewhat faded like it was taken from a security camera, but there was no denying the subject of the photograph. I stared in horror at myself leaning over Lillian's dead body in the basement of the shop earlier tonight. *No Fairy way.*

Finn spoke at my back but his words didn't reach me. The air seemed to leave the room, suffocating me. I scrambled to put the contents of the envelope back inside. My mind could not concentrate on anything but the dreadful warning I received.

Someone knew I was investigating Sylvia and Lillian's deaths—had followed me tonight—and they were not happy about it. I knew that the killer had left this note for me.

My body stood straight as an arrow and my vision

spotted. I had put a target on myself. My thoughts blurred together with only one becoming abundantly clear. The deaths were no accident, and the killer was watching me closely. Worse. They'd been inside my house and I never even knew it.

I was no longer safe in my own home.

Chapter Fourteen

I didn't tell Finn about the letter I received nor the terrible warning inside. I wasn't sure why I kept it to myself, but I hid the envelope as quickly as possible inside one of the kitchen drawers and pretended to think nothing of it. Normally I would let Finn know if I was in any sort of danger, but for some reason, my walls had crawled back up in the last little while, even though I worked hard to tear them down when I met the Wardens. It must have been Rhyven's presence in town. I had to keep reminding myself that no matter how close I had gotten to the Wardens, I couldn't trust anyone.

I was, however, ready to take Finn up on his suggestion to keep ourselves busy. Which was how I found myself back in the town library first thing in the morning.

The morning painted the building in a lovely shade of gold as I pulled my truck into the library's parking lot. As I anticipated, there were only two other cars in the lot. One I recognized to be Finn's and the other I assumed belonged to the librarian on staff today. I was hoping Maggie would not be around so I didn't have to entertain any of her questions. My entire body drooped with relief when I walked in to find a young man at the desk.

Sunlight spilled through a pair of grand arched windows flanking the deep green front door, casting warm patterns across the hardwood floor. The light softened as it touched the surfaces, as if even the sun had learned to tread quietly here. To the right of the entrance, an aged walnut desk sat beneath an ornate chandelier that swayed gently, its glass drops catching the light and sending flickers across the high bookshelves that lined every wall. The shelves, packed with books seemed to breathe as I passed them.

The scent of paper and leather-bound volumes hung in the air. I inhaled it greedily as I made my way to the spiral staircase that coiled upward at the back of the room. The stairs led to a cozy loft, where even more books were shelved in neat, towering rows beneath sloped ceilings. It was also the place where the library stored its computers and archives access and the spot I told Finn I'd meet him in this morning.

He was already seated at one of the stations when I got upstairs.

As I approached him, I remembered our first meeting here in the same library and how hesitant I was to work with the morgue director. It was almost laughable now since I couldn't imagine another person talking about a case to. Especially not one as bizarre as Sylvia's.

"Good morning," I said as I slumped into an empty chair across from a large computer screen.

"Morning to you, too," Finn replied. "Did you get any sleep last night?"

I winced. "Not much. Theo woke me up, begging for food, as always."

"Well, hopefully we can find something here and you can go home to try to get some rest."

We divided the work between us so as not to waste any time. Finn chose to look into Sylvia's history, while I continued my search on Alaric Vionnet, the pattern designer. I scrolled through article after article—from scanned newspaper clippings going back as far as several decades to designer coffee table books. There was more on Alaric here than I could find online which was an excellent start. Unfortunately, aside from the article I'd already read, the rest of the news surrounding the designer focused solely on his work.

Nothing on a possible payday hidden in the crochet pattern.

Clicking out of another dead end, I returned my attention to Finn. "I have nothing," I announced. "Any luck on your end?"

The morgue director shrugged. "Nothing so far. Other than a few social scandals, I can't seem to find a thing that would tie Sylvia to this pattern. Nor to Alaric Vionnet. There's this," he said, pointing at the screen in front of him.

I leaned over in my chair and our elbows brushed against each other. A tingle rushed through my arm. My eyes widened as the warmth of Finn's skin transferred to mine. The hairs on the back of my neck rose from the contact until I was shivering in my chair. Fairy have mercy. It was going to be very difficult to stay professional when this was the kind of physical reaction I had to him. Angling my body in such a way that we couldn't touch, I craned my neck to glance at the screen.

"Content from an estate sale that took place several weeks ago," Finn said.

I pointed to a line on the long list. "A vintage crochet pattern," I said. "This must be where Sylvia found it. She did mention coming across it recently and this estate sale was only a few hours from town."

"That's not the interesting part," Finn said. Scrolling back up the list and clicking on a new tab of the website, he tapped the screen lightly to draw my attention. "You'll never guess whose estate it was."

My eyes narrowed on the words. Shock rattled inside my stomach. *Furlow? This cannot be right.*

"Is there any chance that this was a relative of Edna's?" I asked.

"I double-checked and it appears to be," Finn said.

Hmm.

I considered Edna to be a possible suspect, but she did seem genuinely upset about Sylvia's passing. And if the pattern did belong to her family, surely there were more legal, and less lethal, ways that she could have gotten it back from Sylvia.

"It might be worth it to find out what she was doing at the time of Sylvia and Lillian's deaths," Finn suggested.

I crossed my arms. "She said she was home alone. So, unless there are secret cameras that you have access to from within Edna's home, I don't think we can prove it one way or another."

A sparkle played in Finn's eyes and he wiggled his eyebrows, turning the computer off as he did. "You know what the most frustrating part about living into small town is?" he asked. When I shook my head negatively, he continued, saying, "Everybody always knows each other's business. You can't cross the street without somebody knowing what you're wearing, where you're going, or who you're with."

I chuckled. "I noticed that too. That's why I mostly keep to myself."

"Smart call," Finn agreed. "But today small-town life might actually come in handy, at least for our purposes."

"What are you saying?" I asked the morgue director.

Finn's gaze bore into mine as he asked, "Who needs surveillance footage when you have nosy neighbors?"

Chapter Fifteen

Edna Furlow lived in an idyllic townhome community not too far from Cliff Row, the central street of Orchard Hollow. The townhomes clustered together in between a densely forested area and one of the more private beaches on the long stretch of seaside in our small town. Situated against this wild backdrop, each townhome was exactly the same—a cookie cutter version of its neighbor—but you could see where the residents had added their own flair to differentiate themselves from one another. One front yard was littered with pink flamingos; the plastic kind that you see on beach vacations. Another had a porch that was decorated entirely in a bright shade of lime green starting from the painted railings to the plush chairs that sat upon it. Yet another had an overgrown garden full of vegetables ready for the picking. It was needless to say this one was very much my favorite.

I walked beside Finn as we made our way down the small streets, gawking at every single townhome we passed. A lot of the residents were out and about, and I didn't fail to notice that most of them were of a certain age. Closer to Sylvia and Edna's age than my own.

We reached Edna's townhome, a corner lot with a white picket fence around the front yard, and exchanged twin looks of trepidation before walking past it and heading for the neighboring home. I made sure to double-check that the lights in Edna's townhome were off, to be on the safe side that she wasn't actually around. Following Finn to a bright yellow door, I bit down on my tongue and waited until he knocked lightly before sucking in a calming breath. Finn's idea to question Edna's neighbors looked good on paper when we were back in the library, but now that we were here, about to do the task itself, I seemed to have lost all nerve.

This entire business with a yarn shop made me wish I'd never gotten involved in it in the first place. Yet, it was too late now, and I was smack dab in the middle of things. And yes, I was fully aware that it was my own fault I ended up here, thank you very much.

Finn looked at me over his shoulder and knocked again after there was no reply the first time.

"They might not be home," he said solemnly.

I turned around to inspect the other townhomes surrounding Edna's. Then, raising my pointer finger to single out one directly across the street, said, "Why don't we try that one?"

The door to the townhome was wide open. Surely somebody was home.

We walked down a cobblestone path lined with marigolds and I couldn't help but run my finger alongside one of the petals. In front of me, Finn was completely oblivious to the way the flower reacted to my fairy magic. It stretched in my direction as our energies mingled together. Inside, every ache and fear I may have had before evaporated instantly. It was amazing what nature could do for my fairy soul. I was so entranced in the flowers that I didn't notice Finn stop abruptly in front of me. My forehead collided with his back, eyes watering from the impact. I hissed under my breath, muttering a quick "Sorry" before peering around Finn's wide frame to see what made us stop.

Standing in the open doorway was a person more ancient than some of the royals in the fairy courts. His hair was the color of snow, and he sported a long beard in a matching colorless shade. The man wore a Hawaiian print silk shirt that had several buttons open at the collar to reveal a patch of white dotting his bony chest. He reminded me of a wizard on holiday. I tried not to snicker when the man shook out his hair and his beard bounced so high pieces of it got trapped in his thin lips and it took him several tries to spit it out.

The man placed both his hands on his sides, looking at us incredulously.

"Whatever you're selling, I'm not buying it," he said sternly.

Finn raised his hands in surrender. "We're not here to sell anything, I promise."

"Then why are you littering my front porch?" the holiday wizard asked.

It was at that moment I realized how foolish we must have appeared. Two people who clearly didn't belong here coming up to strangers and questioning them about their neighbor was not going to go over well. Why didn't we think of a better plan before? It never even occurred to me that we might need an excuse as to why we came by. A rookie mistake.

Luckily for both of us, Finn was an expert at the sleuthing business by now. He didn't miss a beat when he said, "Sorry to intrude, sir. Truly. My wife and I are looking to move into the neighborhood and our real estate agent suggested we take the day to talk to the current residents. See if we'd be a good fit for the community."

I sputtered at the mention of being Finn's fake wife and wished I could duck behind him to hide the blush rising to my face. Before I could embarrass myself further, the holiday wizard scowled then dropped his hands from his hips to look us over skeptically.

"Not sure if you noticed, but you're a bit young for this place."

"Oh, we know," Finn said. "It seems like a wonderful community to build a future in. You see, I'm hoping to retire soon and Lyra here ...Well, she's always looking for a slower pace in life, if you know what I mean."

That seemed to have relaxed the wizard. He ran his fingers through his long beard, getting them stuck momentarily before yanking them out. "I certainly do," he said, extending a hand toward Finn. "Young people these days don't understand the power of slowing down, do they?"

"They sure don't, sir," Finn agreed with a chuckle. "My name's Finn O'Malley." He shook the wizard's hand. "This is Lyra, my wife, as I mentioned."

"Dorian Witherall," the man said.

I suppressed another laugh. Even his name sounded like he had magic.

"There are no partying or loud noises allowed here, you understand that?" Dorian said roughly.

We nodded enthusiastically in response.

"We wouldn't dare," I said. "We enjoy our peace and quiet as much as the next person."

Dorian appeared unconvinced, though his expression was a touch less sour than it had been before. Perhaps we were beginning to win the grouchy man over.

"Why this neighborhood in particular?" he asked.

"A friend of a friend recommended it," I said at the same time as Finn said, "Our real estate agent suggested it."

Fairy flowers. Our story was already falling apart, and we hadn't even started yet.

"Well, your friend was right," Dorian said, oblivious to our slip in character. "This is a great area. If you follow the rules and keep to yourself, of course."

"Of course," Finn agreed. He pointed at Edna's house, directly behind us. "We are really hoping for that unit there, but I don't think the owner is going to be selling any time soon."

Dorian barked out a laugh. "Edna? She's not going anywhere. Been here since they built the place. Good luck getting your hands on her place if that's what you were hoping."

"It's a great spot. Quiet and secluded," I said. "Edna is lucky to have it."

This earned me another mocking laugh. "Not so lucky for the rest of us, though," Dorian said.

"Oh?" Finn raised an eyebrow. "How come?"

"Like I said," he continued. "This place is great if

you keep to yourself and follow the rules. Edna here, she does neither of those things."

Finn chuckled. A low and rumbling sound that made my knees buckle slightly. I pushed my attraction for him out of my head before it got me into any trouble.

"I take it Edna is not the quiet type," I said.

"Edna Furlow is the opposite of quiet. She's a thunderstorm. Loud as they can get. Don't know how I got so unlucky as to end up right across the street from her."

I smiled encouragingly. "I would think in a cozy place like this all I'd want to do is stay home and watch TV all day."

"Oh, she sure does enough of that!" Dorian exclaimed.

I scratched my head, pretending to recall a distant memory. "You know, come to think of it," I said, rubbing my temple. "My friend was complaining about some loud noise last Tuesday night. It's probably nothing, but I wonder if maybe the Edna you described is the reason for it."

There was a long silence and I briefly wondered if I laid it on a little too thick, but then Dorian's eyes widened, and an expression of glee took over his face. "That had to be her! I complained to the board the next morning, of course. Could you believe this woman had the TV so loud, watching it right there in her living room with all her blinds open, not caring a bit for the rest of us and disturbing our evening. As if we wanted to watch the Antique Roadshow marathon she had on alongside with her. I came by several times to ask her to turn it down, but she refused to acknowledge my complaints. In fact, I think she even turned the TV louder to annoy me."

"I take it you two don't get along," Finn said.

"You can't get along with a wild boar, Mr. O'Malley."

Boy, Dorian sure seemed to have a thing against Edna. I mean, sure, the woman was opinionated and quite a character, but I couldn't imagine anyone having such a strong animosity towards another human being. Especially over something so silly as a loud television set. How loud could Edna's TV really have been for Dorian to hold a grudge against her? Although maybe it was a collection of small things finally adding up. Dorian struck me as the kind of person who was not exactly easy going, and Edna was the opposite of that. They were two different people living right across the street from each other. Luck was not on either of their sides, it appeared.

My thoughts were cut short when Dorian asked, "What was your friend's friend's name again? The one that lives here?"

I cleared my throat, about to make up some ridiculous name, but before I could make up a lie, Finn took my hand and pulled me backward, saying, "Will you look at the time? We are so sorry to keep you for so long, but you've been most helpful. We're going to tell our agent that this is exactly the kind of neighborhood we want to be in. Nice, quiet, with the type of people that value privacy above all else."

Shuffling his feet, Dorian forgot anything he may have been asking before and nodded approvingly at Finn. "Boy, I sure wished that it was you two living across the street from me and not Edna," he mumbled under his breath, his beard moving up and down as he did.

We hurried out of Dorian's front yard and down the street to where Finn had parked his car earlier. The pair of us couldn't help but want to put more distance between us and the man. Still, as much as I hadn't wanted to come here, it proved helpful. Edna's alibi for the night that Sylvia died was solid. And while that didn't take her off my suspect list, it at least made it less plausible that she was involved.

I kept turning around the conversation with Dorian in my head as we walked until my gaze caught on a familiar face approaching us on the sidewalk. My stomach dropped into my shoes and a sharp breath escaped from my mouth. "Oh no," I whispered.

Finn's eyes narrowed in the direction I was looking. "What is it?" he asked.

My skin blanched.

"That's Dot. Ellie's aunt."

Finn choked on his own saliva. "What is she doing here?"

We slowed our stride, but there was no avoiding the woman nearing us. Judging by her widening smile, she had already spotted me coming toward her. My eyes flicked between her and the other person she was walking with. A woman in her fifties. Before I could even think of an excuse as to why we were here, Dot sped up to close the distance between us.

"Lyra!" she exclaimed. "What are you doing here?"

Once again, Finn came to my rescue because my mouth seemed to be lagging behind my brain and all I did was open it though nothing came out.

"That would be my fault," he said with an easy tone. "I had a package to drop off and dragged Lyra along to keep me company. I'm sure she would prefer to spend the afternoon doing anything but drive around town with an annoying friend."

Dot's eyes traveled over Finn's body to take him in.

"Finn O'Malley, by the way," the morgue director added.

Dot shook Finn's outreached hand with the grip of an anaconda. Her eyes sparkled as she batted her eyelashes in him. "Excellent friends you keep, Lyra."

I shook my head. Then, looking at the woman beside Ellie's aunt, said, "Speaking of friends. Who is this?"

"Why this is Betty," Dot remarked, pointing at the woman. "Our newest crochet club member."

I took in the woman before me, my attention focusing on every detail. She appeared to be quite lovely, with sparkly eyes and silver beginning to thread through her long chestnut hair. She wore it in a loose braid that trailed over one shoulder effortlessly. Her eyes were a warm hazel, a shade I couldn't quite place. Betty appeared to be studying me as intently as I was her which made me drop my gaze to the ground instantly.

I nodded. "Yes, of course, I've heard a lot about you. It's a pleasure to meet you in person."

"Are you in the club as well?" Betty asked.

I squeeze my lips together as Finn chuckled under his breath. Nudging him with my elbow, I said, "No, I'm afraid I don't have the talent you all have for the craft. I am hoping to learn soon. Maybe I might see you around at Tangled Skeins from time to time."

The words fell out of my mouth before I could stop myself. I tried to swallow them again, but the damage was already done. Dot's face darkened and I spotted confusion lacing through Betty.

"I'm so sorry, Dot," I said. "I wasn't thinking."

"It's all right, dear," Dot said, waving me off.

Betty frowned. "What's going on?"

At that, Dot looped her arm under Betty's, leading her away from me and my big mouth. "I'll fill you in during the club meeting," she said, casting a side glance my way to add, "We're having it at Edna's today on account of what happened." She glanced at her watch. "Though we're a bit early. Let's wait for her on the porch. We'll see you later."

As I watched the women speed walk towards Edna's townhouse, the pressure around my chest tightened. I look at Betty's braid as it swayed from side to side while I worried my bottom lip. Someone should warn Betty. I wondered what Dot was going to tell her about Sylvia and Lillian and the death that seemed to stalk the club members. I didn't wish to think so grimly, but at this point, it was really starting to look like the crochet club was cursed. And that anyone who joined it was doomed from the start.

Chapter Sixteen

Sweat beaded and glistened on my brow, trickling down my temple as I leaned into the effort of moving the casket. The polished mahogany gleamed under the flickering sconces, heavy both in weight and meaning. My palms ached against the handles of the wheeled platform as it squeaked its protest across the display room floor. The sound was shrill and jarring, slicing through the thick hush that always seemed to settle over the manor like dust.

From somewhere deep in the bowels of the house, likely the kitchen, where he'd no doubt curled up on a warm windowsill, Theo's voice rang out, muffled but unmistakably irritated. "Keep it down!" he barked, his tone halfway between a hiss and a groan.

I didn't bother replying. The cat had opinions about

everything and contributed very little, unless you counted sarcastic commentary and dramatic sighs as labor. I returned to the task at hand, ignoring him the way one might ignore a creaky floorboard: familiar, constant, and not worth the energy.

Theo was many wonderful things—clever, charming, occasionally insightful—but hardworking was not one of them. He wore laziness like a fine robe, and I suspected it was a trait he'd brought with him from the fae realm, where changelings learned early how to coast by on wit and whimsy. Unfortunately, that didn't help much when actual work needed doing in the human world.

With a grunt, I gave the coffin one final push, sliding it the last two feet into position beneath the soft overhead light. It joined a tidy row of others, each dressed in muted silks and lined with velvet, a quiet display for the dearly departed. Or ones planning for their future.

I stepped back, surveying the arrangement. Mr. Glass was due to arrive within the hour, his aging mother in tow, and I wanted everything to be perfect. Pre-planning a funeral wasn't a task people approached lightly, and I owed it to them to present every option with care. These decisions were about more than wood and lining; they were about legacy, closure, and respect.

When I had the casket I wanted it, I uncurled my spine—it cracked several times—and stretched out my arms overhead. I looked at the display I set up. That should be sufficient for the appointment.

The showroom was the least welcoming room in all of the manor, and I strategically used it for this purpose. It was quiet—too quiet, like the furniture knew to keep its voice down in here. Soft lighting pooled in warm circles above the caskets displayed in rows that lined the walls like a gallery exhibit. The wood ranged from dark mahogany to pale ash, some plain and unadorned, others with brass fittings and delicate carvings of lilies or doves.

To one side, a set of urns stood on glass shelves, varying in style from traditional marble to more modern, artistic pieces—ceramic vessels shaped like hearts, trees, or even ocean waves. A nearby corner featured sample memorial books, sympathy cards, and discreet brochures printed in calming shades of sage and lavender.

Because of everything in here, it was the room that people wanted to spend the least time in. In my experience, people did not want to look at a casket for very long. It truly soured the entire experience of the afterlife.

Since the room had no windows to the outside, I opted for sprawling shelves with fresh potted plants that fell over their planters in green waves. I often got questions about how I kept the plants alive, considering there was no natural light streaming in. Usually, I played dumb and chalked it off to good air flow or some other nonsense that wasn't actually true. In reality, I came down to this room twice a day to feed the plants with my fairy magic. Which was exactly what I was starting to do when the bell at the front door rang out down the hall.

I looked between the shelves of plants and the open doorway behind me. "Sorry," I told the plants. "We'll have to postpone this visit."

Nudging a casket a few inches to straighten it out, I made my way out of the door and walked to the front of the manor. The gargantuan chandelier in the entryway sparkled extra brilliantly too this morning, the rays bouncing off the walls playfully as I walked beneath it. It was so lovely I had almost forgotten my frustrated mood.

After clearing Edna's alibi yesterday, I was getting aggravated with how few leads we were gathering in Sylvia's case. To help matters, I decided to spend the night doing something I hadn't done in a long time—curling up in bed with a good book. It was exactly the type of cozy atmosphere I needed to clear some of my racing thoughts. Except now with the front doorbell continuing to ring, the chaos in my head was back again. I briefly wondered if Mr. Glass had come by early, but from my experience with the man, he was more often late than running ahead of schedule.

I opened the front door, the wood snagging in the frame from the gathering wet heat outside. My body stiffened and my bad mood instantly amplified. My gaze met stormy dark eyes. Before me the Prince of the Shadow Court rocked back and forth on his heels, regarding me with a self-assured smirk and a playful expression. He held out a thick manila envelope my way.

"I got it."

My eyes narrowed on his face. "Good morning to you too, Rhyven."

The prince shook out his perfect locks. "Right. Yes, of course. Good morning. Hope you slept well."

I wasn't sure how this man could go from rude to overly polite in a matter of seconds, but it was funny to see Rhyven squirm a little. It was the closest to seeing him lose his casual and smooth character that I'd seen in ages. I had to admit he did appear to be more relaxed here in the human realm than back in Fairy where he was all spikes and angles.

Still, no matter what act Rhyven was putting on, I could never let myself forget what he truly was: a shadow royal. Not someone to be associated with. Not unless you knew how to play their games and I certainly didn't and didn't wish to learn.

I dropped my shoulders and rolled my eyes. "All right," I said. "I'll bite. What did you get?"

Rhyven nudged his chin at the entranceway. "Aren't you going to invite me in?"

If I could roll my eyes further than I already had, they'd be trapped in the back of my skull. Reluctantly, I opened the door wider, saying, "I suppose you can come in for a bit. I have an appointment in an hour, so I can't dillydally."

Rhyven smirked. "Got it. No dillydallying."

I led him down the winding passages of the manor and toward the living room where Rhyven made himself exceptionally comfortable by collapsing onto the sofa like he owned the place. He rearranged the cushions around him to fully envelop his muscled body, dropping the envelope on the coffee table.

"Check it out."

I inched carefully toward him, bending down to pick up the envelope from the table. "What am I looking at exactly?"

"Background information on every member of the crochet club," Rhyven answered. "Including the two deceased."

My jaw slacked. "H-how did you get this?" I stammered.

"You're not the only one who can make friends with humans, Lyra," he replied.

I didn't want to know who the prince made friends with to get this personal information on the group, and I wasn't about to ask in case what Rhyven did wasn't entirely legal. I wouldn't put it past him to resort to his usual ways in this realm too. Instead, I picked up the envelope and poured the contents out onto the coffee table.

Rhyven was not kidding. There were pages and pages of notes on each single crochet club member. Some so detailed as to document their family histories. Others, like the ones in Aunt Dot's case, had fewer pages. The remainder, like the ones on Lillian, had even fewer pages, but Rhyven did make up for this by providing information on the shop's ownership history. I had to hand it to Rhyven. He sure dug into the club members' info and was more successful than me or Finn.

"Did you happen to find anything to suggest that Lillian had money coming her way? Other than when she bought the shop originally."

"She took out the second mortgage on her house to make that purchase," the prince said. "And she inherited that from her father."

I sighed. Rustling through the papers, I read over the information again. "I'm honestly surprised you even got this far."

Rhyven laced his fingers together and placed them behind his head, crossing his legs as he leaned back comfortably on the couch. His eyes sparkled mysteriously, and he licked his bottom lip before saying, "As I said, I have my ways if you'd ever care to find out for yourself."

I ignored any innuendo, continuing to read through the information he'd provided. Most of the notes were not anything we didn't already know. Edna had lived alone for almost her entire life. Sylvia was married, but her husband died several years back, leaving only her around as they did not have any children. I skipped through some of the sections on Dot since I figured if there was anything truly interesting, Ellie would have mentioned it. I did make note of the fact that she and Sylvia were old schoolmates from college. Not that I considered that to be a key piece of evidence in the case. I already knew they were great friends. That left only one name on the list. A single page. Not nearly as detailed as the others.

I read over Rhyven's careful handwriting, glancing up at him from behind the paper. "You looked into Betty Caldwell?"

"Of course. I know she only recently joined the club, but I wanted to be thorough."

"I met her the other day."

Rhyven folded his arms over his chest. "How was she?"

"Quite lovely," I replied. "It was a brief encounter, so I didn't get a chance to question her about anything. Not that I would. The poor girl. Likely has enough on her hands, what with the new club she joined dying off one by one."

"From what I could dig up, she strikes me as a resilient woman," he said. "Been on her own almost all her life. She had some hardships, but it seems she recovered well." He tipped his chin in the direction of the paper I was clutching. "Sometimes I wonder if being an orphan would have benefited me as well."

Alarm bells rang in my head. I peeled my gaze from prince to look more thoroughly at the page in my hands. I breathed out a low, leveling breath. "She was adopted," I murmured.

"Yes, what of it?" Rhyven asked.

I touched a finger to the tip of my nose, tapping it lightly. "It could be nothing, but when I found Lillian, she was looking into an adoption agency. At first I thought she was looking to adopt, but now? I'm wondering if perhaps she was looking into Betty."

"What was the name of the agency?" Rhyven asked.

I scrambled my brain to remember it, the words slowly coming into focus. "Hope Haven Family Connections," I answered.

"Interesting. That's the same place Betty Caldwell was placed with."

"Did you find—"

Rhyven stopped me before I could finish. "The adoption case was closed. There was no information on the mother nor any information on where she came from. It was, I'm afraid, a dead end."

This new revelation chomped at the back of my brain. Betty was adopted, and Lillian was looking into the same adoption agency. Sure, it could have been a coincidence, but what if there was more to this than we were seeing? I trusted that Rhyven did his due diligence and got whatever he could from the agency itself and if it was as he said, and the adoption was a closed door one, nobody was going to speak to me no matter what I tried.

Unless I went directly to the source.

It may be time to get to know the new crochet club member. If Betty was new in town, who was better to show her around than the local funeral home director?

Chapter Seventeen

Going directly to the source was not as easy as I had originally imagined—mostly because the source was more well-guarded than the state penitentiary.

After jumping through a million hoops—and even employing Rhyven's charm—I managed to convince Ellie to get the most current phone number for Betty from her Aunt Dot. I had to lie through my teeth, of course, to do so, since I couldn't very well tell my friend that I was hoping to possibly scare off her aunt's newest friend with my ridiculous line of questioning.

It took a lot of begging. And a lot of bribing, in other words, promising to bring Rhyven around more when she heard that he was visiting me at the funeral house. Finally, Ellie agreed to help.

And even then, I got nowhere with Betty Caldwell. The woman shut me down before I even had a chance to ask her any of the questions on my list—questions that may have revealed why Lillian was looking into the adoption agency that had placed Betty when she was a baby. She even straight out refused my offer to show her around, telling me point blank that she had no interest in sightseeing. By the end of the call, Betty told me she had urgent plans and couldn't chit-chat for long, brushing me off the phone as though I'd threatened her life.

And while I would love to say that's where I left things ... Unfortunately, with Rhyven in my ear, I continued to press her.

It was that second phone call that really did it. I could hear the fury in Betty's voice when I asked her about the adoption agency. My words blurred together as I struggled to get to the point before she hung up again.

I should've known better than to call a second time, but Rhyven insisted that I do so, telling me we had to get answers one way or another. That we were getting close. There was no telling how he knew our proximity to the truth, because as far as I could see, all we had were empty guesses and leads that led nowhere. That, and a frustrated young woman who told me she didn't wish to discuss her personal life with a stranger and that if I called her again, she'd have to escalate things further.

For all intents and purposes, my first impression on Betty had been an epic disaster.

I hurried Rhyven out of the manor before Mr. Glass and his mother arrived for their appointment, letting him know that if he wished to get more answers, we were going to have to find another way to do so. I wasn't going to ruin my name in town any more than I already had.

After finishing with my appointment, I decided to spend the rest of the day tending to the garden and avoiding any mention of Sylvia or Lillian or the crochet club. The plan was to leave well enough alone while we had the chance.

Considering how little I was able to discern so far—and that threatening note I received the other day—as much as I wanted to find out what happened to Sylvia and Lillian, I had to know when to quit while I was ahead. Or behind, in this case.

My day moved at a snail's pace, and I took on the tasks I often had with less enthusiasm than usual. I didn't like not following up on a lead. But more than that, I didn't like not knowing the truth, especially when I knew there was more to the story than everyone let on.

There had to be another way to find out what had truly happened before somebody else got hurt.

The late afternoon sun bathed the garden in warmth, casting long shadows across the dewy lawn. I slipped on my gloves and made my way toward the rose beds, shears in hand. The bushes were thriving in an explosion of orange hues that looked almost too perfect to touch.

Kneeling beside the nearest bush, I carefully selected a bloom and snipped the stem at an angle. The scent was intoxicating, earthy and sweet. One by one, I clipped my favorites, shaking loose a few stubborn thorns and tucking each stem gently into the basket hooked over my arm.

My wings itched beneath the illusion of magic as I moved through the flowers, their subtle shimmer aching to catch the sun. But I kept the spell firmly in place. There was peace in the garden, even if I didn't feel it inside myself.

By the time I finished, the basket overflowed with blooms. The bouquet was a wild tangle of color and magic, humming against my side as I carried it back toward the house. A flicker of calm passed through me. Even in the middle of confusion and threats and police phone calls ... the roses bloomed.

I carried the lush bouquet inside, kicking off my mud-stained boots at the rear entrance. Taking the bouquet into the kitchen, I found a vase and rearranged the roses. My magic intermingled with that of the flowers, and I sighed, trying hard to remember if I locked the front door.

I glanced around to make sure Theo wasn't nearby. Stripping out of my sweater and down to the tank I wore underneath, I dropped the illusion on my wings that kept them hidden from human eyes. They unfurled behind me, the weight suddenly lifting from my back like I had lost pounds in mere moments. A glitter of rainbow magic surrounded me in a swirl, and I twirled around in it, giggling as my wings flapped slowly. The breeze from their movement made the petals of the flowers shake.

Soon, I was in the middle of a dance in the kitchen, caught in a happiness so pronounced that I could almost taste it. My cheer was short-lived, as my phone rang out on the countertop, making me gasp and retreat my wings back under the hold of the illusion magic. I hiccupped as I looked at the screen.

"This can't be right," I murmured to myself. "Why is the Orchard Hollow police station calling me?"

Was there any paperwork I was supposed to fill out with Sylvia? A piece I missed when I received her body? I didn't think so. I was still waiting to retrieve Sylvia's purse but knowing how backed up the force was, it might be a while until I got it. The police mentioned that they might send Lillian over, depending on what the family wanted, but since I hadn't heard anything since, I assumed her body was already in the hospital morgue. My small funeral home only accommodated so many requests. Space was always an issue, and I was only one person running the show.

Before I could spiral entirely, I picked up the phone, breathing heavily as I said, "Hello? Mistbrook Manor Funeral Home. Lyra speaking."

"Miss Moore?" a voice I didn't think I'd hear again so soon said on the other end. "Officer Brimley here. Not sure if you recall me from the other day."

I gritted my teeth together. "Yes, of course, Officer. How are you today?"

"I'm all right, all things considering."

What things? I wondered.

I didn't have to wonder long before Officer Brimley said, "Listen, I'm sorry to do this. And believe me, I didn't want to call. I'm sure it's nothing, but ... I have to do my job, you understand?"

I didn't understand at all. I had no idea what this phone call was about. Forcing out a smile to try to sound friendlier, I said, "I'm sorry, why are you calling me exactly?"

"I'm going to go ahead and get to it. There's been a report, Miss Moore."

"A report?" My legs trembled, my arm suddenly very heavy. I gripped the phone tightly in my hand. "What kind of report?"

"Well ... there's no nice way to say this. And I truly wish I didn't have to make the call, but Miss Caldwell would like to file harassment charges against you."

I let out an audible gasp. "Harassment? It was two phone calls!"

"She mentioned she never gave you her phone number," Officer Brimley said with a pause.

I flinched. This sure wasn't looking good for me. I had to admit that second phone call was definitely a bad idea. I mentally cursed Rhyven in every uncouth word I could think of in my mother tongue.

"With that said," Officer Brimley continued, "I'm going to go out on a limb here. I assume you didn't intend to harass the lady?"

"I certainly didn't!" I said sharply. "I called to ask her a question about Lillian and the club. I didn't mean anything by it. Honestly, the entire conversation was only a few minutes long. She never let me say what I wanted to say. If I knew she would file for harassment, I never would've made the call. Is there any chance you could speak to her for me? Let her know how sorry I am, and that I promise not to bother her again if she drops the charges?"

There was a brief silence on the other end of the line before Officer Brimley said, "I'll see what I can do. Can't promise anything, but I do believe this was a misunderstanding. Miss Caldwell is new in town—a visitor. She probably isn't accustomed to the way small towns operate."

"And how's that?" I asked.

"You know how it is. Everybody always poking their noses where they don't belong."

The way she said it, so pointedly, I knew exactly what Officer Brimley was saying. Her words made it clear: I needed to stay out of things and not push my luck any more than I already had.

I nodded, even though she couldn't see me. "Of course. I truly am sorry. I won't bother her again."

"I certainly hope not, Miss Moore," Officer Brimley said. "Next time, I'll have to follow through on the claim. I assume that can't be good for someone running a business, can it?"

"Not at all," I agreed. "Thank you for anything you can do to calm things down for me. How are things going with Lillian and Sylvia's cases?"

Officer Brimley hesitated. "How do you mean? Both accidents, as I originally thought. Unless you were able to find anything else on Mrs. Plumwell's body that I should know about?"

I thought back to the silk yarn and the disaster that followed with my half-cocked investigation. Frowning, I said, "Nothing of note."

"As I thought," Officer Brimley said. "Well, I better run. I should make it out to the Rose Hollow Hotel before Miss Caldwell leaves for the day. See if I can straighten this out for you."

The phone hung up as abruptly as it had rung, and for a second, I was left to wonder if any of that had happened at all.

It must have.

I'd really scared Betty off with that disaster of a phone call. I couldn't blame her for getting scared enough to call the police. I must have come off incredibly harsh; especially considering she's new in town and had joined a club where two members died within a week of each other.

What was I thinking?

I grumbled a few more choice words for Rhyven under my breath, then returned to arranging the flowers in the vase on the counter. As I did, I couldn't help but worry my bottom lip, thinking about the terrible impression I had made on Betty.

She was bound to tell Aunt Dot what transpired which meant Ellie would soon find out. I couldn't risk my friend thinking poorly of me over this. Although, knowing Ellie, she'd be more upset that I didn't involve her in the investigation I was running.

Truth of the matter was, I didn't want Ellie involved. I had nothing to go on so far and she was too close to the case. Too close to her aunt and the club. It was a terrible thing to do to a friend. But this terrible thing could blow up to catastrophic proportions if I didn't nip it in the bud right away.

The officer did say that Betty was staying at the Rose Hollow Hotel ...

I thought back to the witch who managed the place with a smile.

As much as I dreaded social interactions, I had to admit, sometimes, it certainly paid to have friends in the right places.

Chapter Eighteen

"Back in an hour!" I shouted as I threw on my shoes and opened the front door.

As soon as I got the go-ahead from Cilia Craven, the witch manager of the hotel, I all but tripped over my own two feet to get to the Rose Hollow Hotel over on Cliff Road.

I half expected Cilia to turn me down immediately, but she seemed fairly open to the idea of letting the information on Betty slip. Especially to confirm that she was, in fact, staying at the hotel and that if I should happen to stop by and accidentally see the room number she was staying in ... Well, such was the case, wasn't it?

I got the feeling that Cilia was used to people like me nosing around. She'd mentioned having a friend that enjoyed a little crime-solving herself in the past and I got the idea that this friend was also keen on prying information from unsuspecting bystanders, perhaps even more so than me.

As I wrestled with my shoelaces, hopping around on one foot to make my way out the door, I prayed that Theo didn't come downstairs to start one of his long monologues about ice cream or whatever else might be on the cat's mind. I wanted to be in and out of the hotel as soon as possible. The plan was entirely clear in my mind: get to the Rose Hollow, find Betty, apologize until my eyes bled, and get the Fairy out. It couldn't have been simpler, really.

That was—until I opened the door and came face-to-face with the two people I least expected to see. At least, not together.

My eyes darted from Finn to Rhyven, standing side by side in front of me.

"Fairy help me," I muttered. "What now?"

I cleared my throat, trying to push away any annoyance from my voice when I said, "Hello, you two."

"Hey," they both said in unison.

Did they practice that?

The glower etched across both men's faces told me everything I needed to know—neither had expected to see the other here. This was no planned encounter, no orchestrated confrontation. Just an unfortunate, painfully awkward coincidence.

Rhyven's eyes narrowed to icy slits, his jaw tight enough to crack stone, the fine tension in his shoulders betraying his sudden shift from relaxed arrogance to razor-sharp wariness. Finn, on the other hand, had gone still in that dangerous, brooding way of his, fists clenched at his sides, a muscle ticking in his cheek as if he were holding back a string of very choice words. The air between them pulsed with the kind of energy that made the hairs on my arms stand on end; a brittle, charged silence that seemed to suck all the warmth from the air.

It might have been laughable, really, if their timing hadn't been so utterly terrible. If I weren't standing between a fae prince who could bend shadows to his will and a man who burned like wildfire when pushed too far, no matter how rare that occasion had been.

And if I weren't utterly exhausted.

The last thing I wanted, truly, the *very* last thing, was to play referee in whatever contest these two seemed to be taking part in. I didn't have the patience, the energy, or frankly, the emotional bandwidth to deal with *either* of them in that moment.

I sighed, slow and deliberate, already feeling the headache forming between my eyes. This was going to be a long day.

"What are you both doing here?" I asked.

"Oh, well, I stopped by to see how you were feeling," Finn said.

"Me too," Rhyven added, his voice stern and commanding.

"Oh," I mumbled. "I'm afraid to say you don't have the best timing. I was actually on my way out for an urgent meeting."

"An urgent meeting?" Finn asked. "What meeting would that be? With whom?"

I really did not wish to lie to the man. Especially not with Rhyven staring me down with daggers in his eyes, as per usual.

"Well, if you must know," I said, looking between the two men, "I was on my way to speak to Betty Caldwell. I wanted to apologize." Then, casting a sharp look at Rhyven, I added, "To stop her from filing a harassment charge against me."

"She's doing what?" Rhyven asked at the same time as Finn exclaimed, "You did what?"

I rolled my eyes skyward. "Yes, well, perhaps you two can catch each other up. I really must go if I have any chance of fixing this before it goes too far."

I started to brush past them when Rhyven caught my arm, spinning me around to face him. "You mean to say you found out where she's staying?"

"I thought that was clear," I replied.

"And you're going to barge in on her even though you're worried she might go to the police?" Finn asked.

"I mean ... when you put it that way ..." I trailed off.

The Shadow Prince and the morgue director glared at me like I was speaking in tongues. Exasperated, I slapped my hands against my thighs. "What would you have me do? I can't have her ruin my reputation. There was clearly a misunderstanding."

"Or ..." Rhyven said.

"Or?" I spun around to face him, Finn doing the same. "Or what?"

The Prince of the Shadow Court shrugged, curving one eyebrow in my direction. "Since you know where she's staying, we could use this opportunity to find out if she's up to no good."

I groaned. "Not this again."

"I hate to admit it, but I think I agree with the man," Finn said.

I must have heard incorrectly. Shaking my head, I crossed my arms and turned to the morgue director. "Are you serious?"

"Sadly, yes. As much as I don't want to get you into any more trouble," Finn continued, "and I really don't want to agree with whatever plan your friend here may have created in his head ... from what I've been told, Betty Caldwell sounds like she's hiding something."

My eyes narrowed. "From what you've been told? By whom?"

A flash of Rhyven's teeth blinded me in my peripheral vision.

Of course. How long had these two been standing out here and chatting without me knowing it? I really could not handle them becoming friends. Not when I was trying to keep both of them out of my life for fear of the complications it caused.

I glared at them.

They glared back.

None of us budged.

Glancing at my watch, I realized time was ticking. Cilia wasn't going to wait around forever. I wasn't about to agree to anything Rhyven came up with, but at this point, I would miss my chance to apologize to Betty, and I couldn't afford to take that risk. I blew out a breath, a wayward strand of hair fluttering across my forehead.

"Ah. Fine," I finally ordered. "Let's go. But no one does anything unless I approve. Got it?"

Finn smiled while Rhyven winked. "Sounds good, boss," the prince said.

"You two go. I'll follow you in my car," Finn suggested.

And just like that, my day got a whole lot more complicated.

We arrived at the Rose Hollow Hotel right on time. As we stepped through the revolving glass doors, warmth wrapped around me like a velvet curtain, muffling the outside world. The floor beneath me was polished mahogany, nearly hidden by a richly patterned rug that muffled my footsteps. To the right, a quaint lounge area featured two vintage loveseats with carved wooden legs, facing each other across a low table of dark walnut. A handful of guests were scattered there, flipping through glossy brochures or scrolling on their phones in silence, though they all appeared to be on their way out. Beyond the lounge, an old-fashioned elevator stood out from the wallpapered walls, its bronze latticework glinting under the amber lights. A luggage cart waited nearby while a bellhop in a tailored crimson jacket carefully loaded bags, nodding in greeting when he spotted us entering.

Cilia was waiting for me at the front desk, like she did the first time I came around here. Her short blonde bob was effortlessly styled today, and she wore a heavy liner on her upper lids, making her stare all that much more intimidating. As we approached, Cilia darted her gaze between me and the men stalking on either side of me, her brows arching higher and higher with each step that cleared the distance between us. The sound of the thundering pulse between my temples was impossible to ignore, and I almost didn't hear her when she said, "Didn't realize you were coming with an entourage." Cilia chuckled. "Quite the set of bodyguards you have."

I laughed sheepishly. "Not my first choice of company today," I mumbled under my breath. "Sorry to barge in on you like this. And thank you for any help you can provide. I mean that, really."

"Like I mentioned before," Cilia said, "I can't help all that much." Her tone rose slightly when she uttered the words I read between the lines instantly.

"Of course," I agreed. "I completely understand."

Cilia angled the laptop set up on the counter on the reception desk toward me.

"Maybe you can tell me how all that business at the funeral home has been going."

She purposely looked away, and I got the drift immediately, nudging Rhyven in his side so he could take the opportunity to glance at the room number listed under Betty Caldwell's name. While the prince did what he did best, skulking in the shadows, I entertained Cilia with tall tales from Mistbrook Manor Funeral Home. I told her every detail I could imagine, no matter how unimportant it may have seemed. Basically, I talked until I was blue in the face.

When Rhyven finally stepped away from the laptop,

nodding at me to let me know he got what we needed, I finished my pointless recounts of the day, smiled at Cilia and said, "It was really great seeing you again."

"You too," the hotel owner replied. "We should make this a social thing next time."

Agreeing to meet her later, I let the woman pack up her things and walk away, leaving only the three of us in the now surprisingly empty hotel lobby.

I looked at Rhyven. "Did you get it?"

"Did you have any doubt?" he said quickly. "Now, before you go off and do something you'll probably regret later, do you mind if I use the little boys' room?"

My eyes narrowed at the prince. "I suppose we can wait for a bit. But don't take too long, I don't want to hang around here longer than needed, and I really do want to get this over with."

"Will do, boss," Rhyven said.

I watched him disappear down one of the corridors jutting away from the main reception area, his shoulders rigid and the muscles of his arms and legs rippling as he walked.

Next to me, Finn hummed. "Interesting guy," he said.

"He sure is," I replied.

Finn's expression soured mildly. "So ... how do you two know each other?"

The thought of telling Finn about my sordid history

with the Prince of the Shadow Court gave me hives. I scratched my skin, crawling out of it as I thought about everything I was hiding from the morgue director. There was absolutely no way I could tell Finn the truth. And it bothered me that I couldn't be more open with him. It was a constant reminder that, no matter how close we could get, there would always be truths I'd have to hide from him.

Where I'm from, for starters. My magic. And then the business with my arranged marriage to Rhyven.

"It's a really long story," I said instead of explaining anything.

"Maybe you could tell it to me one day when you're ready," Finn suggested.

I pressed my lips together. "Yes. Maybe one day. Thank you for being so understanding."

"It's not a problem," Finn said. "I—"

His words were cut off by the sound of feet shuffling rapidly as they neared us. We both stopped short, spinning around to face the direction we'd seen Rhyven disappear in not so long ago. The Prince of Shadows came running toward us like he was being chased by a mob. His eyes were wild, and his hair was mussed, bouncing as he moved faster and faster in our direction. A panic rose within me, and I swallowed it down, knowing full well that whatever Rhyven had to say, I wasn't going to like it.

The prince skittered to a stop a few inches before me, his breath shallow.

"What happened?" I asked.

"We should probably go," Rhyven said, collecting himself.

"What did you do?" Finn scolded.

The prince rubbed his chin, his head cocked to the side. "Saved you the trouble of having to apologize. I may or may not have gotten into Betty's hotel room."

"You did what?!" Finn and I asked in unison.

Rhyven brushed us off. "I did what I had to do so the rest of you didn't get into any more trouble," he explained. "And believe me when I tell you—it was worth it."

I wanted to scold him. I wanted to lash out and tell him exactly what I thought about what he did, how much jeopardy he was putting me and my position in this town in. My entire livelihood. I wanted to ...

I stopped, sighing. "Tell me what you found."

"Oh, nothing major. Only Betty Caldwell's real identity. And this."

He reached into his blazer and pulled out a wrinkled photocopied page.

"What is that?" I asked.

Finn looked over my shoulder to glance at the paper. "That looks like a crochet pattern."

Rhyven wrinkled his nose at the morgue director.

"Say, how good are you at deciphering hidden messages?"

Finn glanced at the photocopy of the pattern in my hands, then back at Rhyven. "I'm decent with it. And if I can't crack it, I know a few people we can call."

I didn't have to ask him to know that the people he was referring to were the Grim Wardens. As much as I didn't want to get them involved right now, what I didn't want more was for Betty to come crashing down into the lobby to catch us standing here with something that clearly belonged to her.

Although ... how did she get this?

"Whatever questions you've got in that busy brain of yours," Rhyven said, "we should probably leave."

"Why?" I asked.

"Remember how I said I may or may not have ended up in Betty's room?"

I nodded.

"Well, I also may or may not have been caught by one of the staff. So, unless you want to get arrested right now, I would hustle."

Before I knew it, Finn and Rhyven each grabbed one of my arms and hauled me toward the door. My legs twisted out from under me, and I almost tripped several times, needing Finn to help hoist me back up so I didn't faceplant right there in the hotel lobby. There was a slight commotion behind us, and I knew that whoever caught Rhyven in Betty's room was about to call security. Which meant Cilia would certainly find out what he did.

I couldn't think about that right now.

The hotel owner struck me as someone who understood what it meant to solve a case. And if not ... well. That was another relationship I'd have to repair, thanks to the Prince of the Shadow Court. I continued to mumble under my breath as we rushed from the hotel and to our respective cars, hoping that I could leave the entire day behind me.

Though, considering what Rhyven said he discovered, and the copy of the crochet pattern now clutched in my hands, there was no leaving this behind anymore, was there?

This was it. We were on to something. I could feel it. Now, whether that something was going to land me in jail? That was a whole other story.

Chapter Nineteen

The sound of voices and cups clinking faded into the background as we sat in the Whistling Kettle with several teacups sitting between us, along with the adoption papers stolen from Betty's room and laid out like a map on the table. I stared at them, rereading the names assigned on the page over and over again. As though each time I read them, I would see a different name show up.

But it was always the same.

And my disbelief only multiplied with each second. Even now that we knew who Betty Caldwell really was, I still couldn't see the resemblance. They were so different. Then again, people did change as they grew older. And maybe I couldn't see it because I didn't want to believe it. The only thing they had in common were those warm hazel eyes which really wasn't much if you thought about it. And yet ...

Betty was Sylvia's daughter.

According to the paperwork, Sylvia gave her up for adoption. There was no reason stated, but judging by the year of birth Sylvia listed for herself, I assumed she was too young to care for her child. There was no father mentioned in the adoption papers, which led me to believe she likely gave up her baby to give her a better life. Looking at the way events unfolded later, it appeared that Betty was not all too pleased about it.

"I feel like I'm acting out the script in a movie," I told the men. "It's so unbelievable."

"That Betty was Sylvia's daughter?" Finn asked. "Or that she killed her?"

I grimaced. "Both."

At the far end of the table, Rhyven took a long sip of his tea, putting the cup down with a clank. I didn't fail to notice the three women sitting at the table next to us stared at him so intently that I could swear I saw drool drip from the sides of their mouths. Rhyven seemed completely oblivious to being the center of attention. His gaze focused entirely on me when he said, "It's not all that unbelievable, considering the situation she found herself in."

I arched a brow in his direction. "What situation was that?"

"While I was in the room, there was other paper-work lying about. I didn't get to grab it on account of being caught red-handed and all, but it looks like there are a lot of debts hanging over Betty's head. I'm willing to bet she was in quite the financial turmoil. Which might explain why she killed Sylvia."

"Still," I murmured, "to kill your own mother for money? Isn't that too extreme?"

"I doubt she saw Sylvia as a mother figure," Rhyven suggested. "The woman gave her up when she was a baby. Perhaps her trouble was too dire, and she saw no other way out."

I couldn't accept that. Pulling my finger around the rim of the cup, I said, "Couldn't she simply ask Sylvia for help? I hadn't known Sylvia for very long, but she didn't strike me as a malicious person. Certainly not someone who would turn her back on her own child."

"She turned her back on her before," Rhyven said.

"We don't know why she did it," Finn said quietly. "It's not up to you to judge her. If you want to judge anybody, judge the killer."

"We also don't know if that's truly the case," I said. "But you're right. This doesn't give us anything we can bring to the police. And if we want to prove that Betty killed Sylvia and Lillian," I added, my voice lowering, "we need a confession."

A few more cups clinked around us. The sound of

high-pitched laughter from a few tables over made me cringe. Clearly, this was much too public a place for this discussion. We needed to be somewhere away from prying eyes, but only two places came to mind.

One was the manor—and I had no intention of bringing both Rhyven and Finn back to my house. Especially not with Theo there or I'd never hear the end of it. That left the Grim Wardens' secret library under the mausoleum, and while it was a wonderful place to discuss cases, I certainly couldn't tell Rhyven about it. Not without betraying the trust of the others.

I looked around the packed teahouse. I supposed this would have to do for now.

My thoughts raced a mile a minute as I tried to think of the next step we could take. The more I thought about it, the more I realized that we were stuck between a rock and a hard place. Betty had already threatened to follow through with harassment claims. She'd made it very clear I was not to approach her again. And now, with Rhyven breaking into her room, surely she'd be on high alert even if she wasn't already fleeing town. We needed to find another way to get close to her. To get a confession.

And we had to do it fast.

Time was quite literally running out.

I took a tiny bite of a cucumber sandwich, the taste barely registering in my mouth. "I have no idea how we're going to do this," I said. "Betty won't agree to meet with anyone she doesn't trust right now."

"Then make her feel she has no choice," Finn said.

I stopped chewing and put the sandwich down, turning to look at him. "How do you mean?"

"Well," the morgue director said, "if she won't come to us, perhaps we can force her to by making her feel she has no choice." He tapped his finger on the photocopy of the crochet pattern. "You said the pattern wasn't among Sylvia's belongings at the funeral home, correct?"

I nodded slowly. "No. I assumed the killer took it. Knowing what I know now about Betty, I'm willing to bet she has the original."

"Then why have a photocopy of it?" Rhyven asked.

Finn flipped the copy of the pattern on the table. "Exactly. The only reason she'd own a copy is if she hid the original. If Lyra is right, and this thing is worth as much as we believe it is, I wouldn't want it lying around a hotel room either."

Rhyven planted his elbows on the table and leaned in closer to us. "What are you suggesting we do?"

"I'm suggesting," Finn said, "that you get back to the crochet club you're a new member of."

When Rhyven's eyebrows shot up, Finn added, "Please. Spare me the performance about your under-cover infiltration. I have to say, I'm impressed. We could definitely use your standing with the club to get what we need."

"How do you figure?" Rhyven's eyes blazed.

"As far as Betty and the other ladies are concerned, you're new in town. They don't know your connection to Lyra, or that you're helping us with this case."

"Helping *her*," Rhyven corrected, "with Sylvia and Lillian's case."

"I'm thinking that if you go back to the club and casually mention that the police found the pattern—and they're tracing fingerprints on it—it might be enough to throw Betty into a panic."

"You want to force her to retrieve the original copy," I said.

Finn smiled. "It's a long shot. But it might work."

"Even if you do force her hand," Rhyven said, "how would we know where she'd go? We don't know where she hid the original pattern."

"That's true," Finn agreed. "Though ... there couldn't be too many places to search, could there? Betty doesn't know much about this town. There are only a few places she's been since she got here. I say we station ourselves at the most plausible areas. The hotel room. Sylvia's home—which I assume she's been watching—and ..."

"The yarn shop," I said quickly. "It would make for a good hiding place."

"The shop *has* been closed since Lillian's death," Finn added. "That makes it the perfect spot to stash the pattern until she's ready to return for it."

"Then that's our plan," Rhyven said, pushing back his chair. "Everybody take a location, and we go from there."

"Are you sure you're all right to spread the rumor at the club?" I asked.

Rhyven cracked his knuckles, the corner of his mouth ticking upward. "Of course, darling," the prince purred. The hairs on my arms stood straight up. "I've been playing a role my entire life. This'll be a piece of cake."

Chapter Twenty

I huddled behind the kitchen counter in the dark, dank apartment Lillian kept behind Tangled Skeins. Every shadow bouncing off the walls made my body shiver. I glanced at my watch, wondering how long I'd been here. It felt like hours, but in truth, not all that much time had passed.

The police tape was still across the front door of the apartment, invisible to any passerby outside, since it was in the rear of the shop. Yet I knew what happened here not all that long ago.

Images of Lillian's dead body in the basement flashed before my eyes. I shuddered, pushing them away and removing any trace of fear I may have felt. Now that I was here, I regretted coming alone. I was the one who agreed to spread out, but somehow, I had the distinct feeling that if Betty hid the pattern anywhere, it would be here in the shop. It would make the most sense. If she did, in fact, confront Sylvia and kill her for the pattern then leaving it here, hiding it in plain sight, would be the best solution.

Especially if she hurried to get out before the police arrived.

It might also explain what happened with Lillian and why Betty returned to the scene of the crime.

A rustle outside the apartment made me stop breathing for a moment. I listened, ears alert for any sound of life other than my own, but the apartment remained eerily quiet. If Betty was coming, she certainly wasn't here yet.

As I waited, I tried to imagine what Rhyven and Finn were going through, and wondered if they were as worried as I was. Somehow, I doubted that the Prince of the Shadow Court held any fear and Finn always appeared so cool and collected, entirely put together. Completely ready to confront a killer.

The thought of Betty killing her own mother made bile rise in my throat. I coughed into the palm of my hand, resting my back against the grimy wall behind me and ignoring the stickiness on my clothes it left behind. There was another rustle outside, followed by the jiggling of a handle.

My breath caught. Someone was here.

My body shook with adrenaline as the front door creaked open. The singular light bulb outside illuminated some of the apartment and I ducked down further to stay out of sight. A shadow in the shape of a person elongated toward me. It grew larger and larger as whoever was in the apartment walked further in. Blood rushed from my face, and a clammy coldness spread over my skin.

This was it.

I sucked in a trembling breath, my eyes widening as the shadow inched inward. The sound of heavy footsteps echoed through the empty space, and their vibration made my heart race like a galloping horse. I regretted every decision I made that led me to this point. The light from outside lit the figure in a faint golden hue, and the tension in my muscles lessened when my eyes focused on who it was.

"Rhyven?" I said, surprised. "What are you doing here? You're supposed to be watching the hotel."

The prince strolled toward me. His hair was mussed, like he'd rushed to get here. He ducked around the counter to join me in my hiding spot, keeping his voice low "Betty left the hotel not long ago," he said in a hushed tone. "It appeared she was heading this way, but I lost her in a crowd of people. I figured since there was no point in me staying at the hotel, I may as well come and make sure you were all right. In case she did make her way over here."

I was about to thank him when another sound caught my attention from the front door.

"Hello?" a voice sounded through the dark apartment. "Is anyone here?"

I clutched Rhyven's arm. "Did you leave the front door open?"

Rhyven winced.

I rolled my eyes, smacking his arm lightly. "At this point," I muttered, "we may as well be holding up a sign that says *This is a trap—don't come any farther.*"

Not far from us, the sound of footsteps grew louder as the newcomer made their way further into the apartment. Though I'd only spoken to her on a few short occasions, there was no mistaking the voice.

Betty Caldwell was here.

I looked at Rhyven, my gaze meeting his behind the counter. "It's her," I mouthed.

Rhyven shot me a thumbs-up but stayed quiet.

"Hello?" Betty asked again.

Slowly, I inched further into the shadows of the kitchen, urging Rhyven to follow. We stayed in complete silence, hoping that Betty couldn't hear us before she did what she came here to do. I supposed the draw of a possible fortune was more pressing than checking every nook and cranny of the apartment, because the next thing I knew, there was the sound of something dragging and the shuffling of things in the living room.

I looked at Rhyven, who nodded before shifting a smidge so I could sneak by him. Moving at a snail's pace, I kept every movement slow and light as I pushed my head around the side of the counter to peer into the living room. Betty stood with her back to me, facing the dirty old couch I'd seen here before. One of the cushions was turned over and laying on its side on the floor beside it. She rummaged in the crevices of the couch, pulling out a few yellowing papers. She unfolded them, glancing at the pages in her hand.

I didn't have to get a closer look to know what it was.

You were right after all, I thought. *Betty did take the pattern from Sylvia—and hid it here to collect it later.*

I backtracked to make my return to Rhyven. As I did, my foot slipped on the floor and slammed into the side of the counter with a loud thud. My eyes sprang open as Betty twisted on her heels to face me, a gasp falling from her lips. She glared at me through the dim light of the apartment, venom in her stare.

"You," she said coolly. "What are you doing here?"

I glanced from her to the pattern in her hands. "I could ask you the same question," I said. "Though I think we both know the answer to that."

"Why are you even here?" Betty howled. "What is your obsession with following me?"

I nearly choked on the laugh that bubbled up from within me.

"You're kidding, right?" I said. "You are quite literally standing in the crime scene with a stolen pattern in your hands, the one that you got after killing your own mother, and you're asking *me* why I'm here?"

Betty's expression turned to ice. "I don't know what you think you know," she said, "but you've made a terrible mistake coming here."

"What I know is that you killed Sylvia, your own biological mother, for that pattern. I think you know there's a hidden message in it, left by Alaric Vionnet, and you were hoping to cash in on it. And I think that Lillian was on to you, so you followed her here under the pretense of wanting the apartment and pushed her down the stairs before she could tell the police what she knew."

Betty worked her jaw as she looked me over.

"That's actually not too far off," she said, a sly grin playing on the edges of her lips. "Though I didn't follow Lillian," she corrected. "She already offered me the apartment. I had a key and everything. All I had to do was wait for the right time. I had no idea she was digging around in my past. I actually came by to return the key to her and to tell her I was leaving town, but then I caught her looking into the adoption agency. The fall was an accident."

"Yeah, right," I said.

"It was. I tried to talk to her to clear things up and let her know what happened. That I wasn't the bad guy here. I wasn't the one who left her kid to fend for herself."

I scowled. "You have no idea why Sylvia did what she did. Did you even ask her why she put you up for adoption before you killed her?"

"Why would it matter?" Betty exclaimed. She slammed her hands on her thighs, crinkling the pattern pages in the process. "She left me alone. I tried to reach out to her a long time ago. She made it very clear that she wanted nothing to do with me. Then, after the divorce, when my pathetic ex-husband left me with nothing to my name, I reached out again asking for help. You know what she did?"

I didn't answer. As much as I didn't want to imagine Sylvia being so cruel, I had a feeling I knew where this was going.

"She told me not to contact her again," Betty said. Her voice grew hoarse. The darkness danced in her eyes. For a moment, it looked more like sadness.

I shook my head, my brow creasing. "That was not a good enough reason to kill her," I said firmly.

"I didn't mean to kill her," Betty said. "She was

boasting about that pattern and how much it was worth all over the town. I overheard her and Edna arguing about it several times in public when I followed her discreetly. It was pathetic. I was one step away from losing everything and here she was, sitting on a payday and refusing to help her own kid. All I did was ask her to help me out. I told her we could sell the pattern together. That I only needed enough to get by, but she refused to hear anything of it. I'm sure you won't believe me, but when I came to talk to her that night, all I wanted was for her to listen. It didn't quite work out that way, though."

My body stilled, listening. Lowering my brows, I cast Betty a disdainful look. "Then how do you explain strangling her with the silk yarn?"

The blood drained from the woman's face as she regarded me carefully. Her shoulders hiked up and she swallowed several times, not speaking a word.

I rolled my eyes. "There goes your sob story about it being an accident. Can't exactly accidentally strangle someone, can you?"

My head spun as I considered Betty's story. On one hand, two women were dead because of her own selfish needs. On the other, I couldn't imagine being in her position—confused and desperate with someone you wanted to accept you telling you to leave. She didn't deserve what happened to her. Sylvia certainly didn't. Yet I couldn't help but feel sorry for Betty and what she'd gone through in her life. Until I thought about that Fairy cursed silk yarn.

I opened my mouth to speak, to talk some sense into Betty before she did something else she'd regret, but a sharp clicking sound cut through the air, stopping me in my tracks. My eyes darted to the gun in Betty's hand. *Where did she get that from?* I hadn't even seen her move.

She pointed the gun in my direction. "Really sorry. But I can't let you leave here."

"You don't have to do this, Betty," I said, voice quivering.

"I'm afraid I do," the woman remarked, finger pressing on the trigger.

I shut my eyes, bracing for what came next, when a whooshing sound passed by my ears. My eyes flew open to follow it. Deep shadows stretched from behind me and toward Betty. The woman's finger paused on the trigger, and her eyes widened in horror as Rhyven's magic blasted toward her. The shadows collided with her chest, throwing her backwards so hard she flew halfway across the room, her back slamming into the hard wall. The breath knocked out of her, and she screamed before collapsing down onto the floor. Betty's eyes fluttered as she looked at Rhyven with complete and utter terror. She started to crawl for the gun that had dropped a few feet from where she lay.

Rhyven raised a finger in the air, stopping her. "I wouldn't do that if I were you," the Prince of the Shadow Court warned.

Somewhere outside, the sound of sirens blared to life. Flashing lights reflected through the small window at the front of the apartment. I twisted my neck to gape at Rhyven, a questioning look on my face.

"I had your friend call the police before I came here," Rhyven explained. "I figured you'd want to handle this the human way."

Not bothering to ask him how else he would've handled it, I rushed over and kicked the weapon farther out of Betty's reach, then returned to join Rhyven. "She might tell someone what she saw," I whispered.

Rhyven's eyes grew stormy.

"Let her try," the prince said. "I have a feeling, considering the murder charge against her, no one will believe a word that comes out of her mouth."

The sirens grew louder in the distance, and the sound of boots hitting the ground surrounded us as the police made their way through the alley leading to the apartment. Though Betty kept her expression neutral, her jaw clenched tightly, and her eyes narrowed on me and Rhyven.

I couldn't help but feel sorry for her. That was the thing about murder. At the end of the day, whether you were caught or not, nobody truly won.

Did they?

Chapter Twenty-One

I stood between Finn and Rhyven, watching a crowd of people huddle around the entrance to Tangled Skeins. Ever since news got out about what happened to Sylvia and Lillian, people had been popping by the shop—whether to gawk at the crime scene or to pick out yarn, nobody truly knew.

There were a few tourists taking candid photos of the place. Some were more candid than others, and I couldn't help but shake my head at them. The macabre always attracted an audience, didn't it?

I watched as Dot, Ellie, and Edna walked up to the front door. Ellie smiled as Dot pulled out the shop keys and opened the door, flipping the "Closed" sign around to let people know that Tangled Skeins was officially open for business again.

The entire thing was nothing short of a miracle.

After several tries, Finn and the Wardens managed to decode the secret message in the pattern, and as it turned out, Alaric Vionnet was not simply putting on a show. The pattern *did* lead to a safety deposit box in one of the banks in town; one complete with the will to his estate and trust, and the rights to his design business.

It wasn't as much money as Betty thought, certainly not enough to kill for. But there was plenty there to keep the shop afloat. And since the pattern technically belonged to both Edna and Sylvia, the ladies decided to use the funds to keep the shop open in Sylvia and Lillian's memory by buying it from the estate.

It was a lovely gesture and an excellent business call, considering the people now pushing their way through the entrance to go inside.

"Quite the crowd," Rhyven noted as several more people crammed into the small shop.

"Certainly busier than it's ever been before," I agreed, glancing at the prince. "Are you thinking of joining the crochet club again?"

Rhyven chuckled. He smiled, his gaze focused on the shop windows. "I might. It'd be an excellent way to pass the time while I'm in town."

"Are you staying for a while?" Finn asked.

There was a slight animosity in his voice, but it wasn't as pronounced as before. It appeared that working together had put the two men quite at ease with each other and I thoroughly appreciated the fact that I could spend time with both of them around. Even though I had decided not to follow through on any romantic feelings with Finn, nor the confusing ones I had for the prince. My life was simply too chaotic at the moment to worry about romance. And while both men surprised me—both of them having positive traits I couldn't get out of my mind—there were too many cons for me to get tangled up in any romance at the moment.

Being with Finn might prove much too difficult, since I could never really be myself around the human. At least, not fully. And, while Rhyven knew who I was, knew of my fae heritage, I couldn't get past everything his family stood for.

Besides which, I wasn't sure I could ever return to Fairy.

I loved my life in Orchard Hollow. It was one I built for myself, and I was proud of everything I'd accomplished here. Not to mention the Grim Wardens, whom I had grown quite fond of. So, for now, I decided to stay put and keep things as they were while also keeping the men at arm's length. I was hoping they'd both be all right with that decision.

"I do like it here," Rhyven said, replying to Finn's earlier question. "A lot to do in Orchard Hollow. When you're not solving murders, that is," he quickly added.

Finn laughed.

"We certainly have enough of those to go around," he said. "Though I suppose that comes with the careers we've chosen for ourselves."

I looked between the two men, then back at the shop window, noticing Ellie waving at us to come in from inside. My chest warmed. As we walked into the shop, it came to life around me. The coziness and peace that Tangled Skeins had offered on my prior visits was replaced by something more alluring and much more addictive.

Excitement.

Happiness and laughter echoed through the space, bouncing off the walls and the skeins of yarn that filled the baskets of every customer inside. What happened to Sylvia and Lillian in the shop was tragic and unnecessary, but it brought new life to the store, and I couldn't help but smile at the pure joy on Dot and Edna's faces. The ladies worked in unison to serve every client who walked through the door, their eagerness to talk about yarn and crocheting so evident it radiated off them. This was the kind of memory that both Lillian and Sylvia would want to leave behind—people loving the same thing they loved, as thoroughly as they did.

And with Betty arrested and awaiting trial, it never felt safer to be here.

As much as I empathized with Betty and the harsh

turns her life took, I knew there was no way she was ever going to see life outside of a jail cell. The evidence was simply too stacked against her. The only thing I hoped for was that the woman would feel some sort of remorse for what she did. At least attempt to understand that her actions did not bring any justice; not in the way that she was hoping for. There was really no way to know why Sylvia gave up her baby all those years ago, and all we could do was guess at the reason for it. But she didn't deserve to die. That was not how the scales of balance worked.

"Would anyone like a cup of tea?" Ellie yodeled from the front counter.

A few hands shot up instantly, and as I turned around, I noticed a new group of people sitting in the center of the room, crochet hooks and projects in hand. My lips split into a wide smile as I watched them chatter while working on their pieces.

The shop was so lively, it was almost as though Sylvia and Lillian were here. If I believed in the afterlife or ghostly apparitions, I knew I'd see them standing in the corner, their own crochet hooks clutched in their fingers, gossiping about one thing or another alongside the new group.

Life went on, whether we were ready for it or not.

I looked at Finn. Then shot my gaze over to Rhyven, as I bent over to pick up a spare crochet hook from one of the tables. I grabbed a ball of yarn, tossed it in the air, and caught it again, my eyebrows wiggling.

"I think I might crochet for a while," I announced. "Who wants to join me?"

With the business of the yarn shop out of the way, and Sylvia and Lillian's cases closed, I could finally concentrate on the other problem that had me tossing and turning at night. My brow was slicked with sweat as I twisted my magic right and left, attempting to open the portal to the ice world. So far, nothing did the trick. I even went as far as visiting my original portal site to Fairy back at the cemetery, to see if the energy there could be of any use. But much like here in the manor, I couldn't get the doorway to show up—let alone open.

Must be something I'm missing.

Surrounding me, the orange-hued roses bristled in the light wind. The briar thorns crawled toward me slowly as the flowers responded to my magic. I threw another burst of it out again before checking on Theo, who was fast asleep on the wooden bench near me.

"Well, that's new," a familiar voice said behind me.

I dropped the hold of my magic, letting it dissipate

into the earth, and turned around to face Rhyven standing in the back. Smirking.

"Hi, Rhyven," I said. "I keep at it, but I haven't had any luck yet."

The prince stalked toward me, the buttons of his white shirt straining with every step. He knelt on the ground, crouching beside me, and said, "I think it's time I told you how I got to this realm."

My eyes widened, and excitement rumbled through me. "Yes, please!" I exclaimed. "Maybe if I knew how you opened the portal, I could use that to figure this out."

Rhyven grimaced. *Oh no.* "That's the thing, Lyra," he said quietly. "I didn't open the portal."

"Then how did you get here?" I asked.

One side of Rhyven's lips quirked upward. "I followed you. I came through the same one that you came through."

"Wait, what?"

That couldn't be right. I had been on Earth for over a decade. If Rhyven followed me through the portal, that would mean ... "You've been here this whole time?"

Rhyven nodded.

"Why didn't you come to see me sooner?"

He shrugged, rubbing his forehead and looking slightly past my left shoulder. "As I said before, the timing wasn't right, and I didn't want to scare you. I really am trying to earn your trust, Lyra. I don't want to do anything to hurt you. And ... you seemed really happy here. I figured if I showed up, I might ruin that for you. But then ..."

I recalled our first meeting here on Earth.

"Then I got myself in trouble, and you had to come save me."

Rhyven growled deep in his chest. "I couldn't let that horrible man hurt you," he said.

As the realization of what he was saying finally hit me, my shoulders slumped, all the fight draining out of me like someone had pulled the stopper in a bathtub. I rocked back on my heels, knees wobbling, and then let gravity take over, sitting my bum in the dirt with a soft thud. The ground was cool beneath me, gritty and uneven, tiny pebbles pressing into the skin through the thin fabric of my pants. I didn't care.

The world around me blurred at the edges, not from magic this time, but from the weight of understanding settling over me like a wet wool blanket. I curled my fingers into the soil, needing something solid to hold on to, something real. My heart pounded in that heavy, aching way it does when hope flickers and goes out.

I stared ahead, not really seeing anything. Just trying to make sense of it all. The words kept echoing in my head, louder than the wind, louder than the distant hum of life continuing without me. And all I could think was:

So, this is how it ends. Not with a bang. But with a sentence.

"That means this is totally useless. I'm never going to be able to open this portal," I said. "And I'm never going to figure out what's wrong with my magic."

"Not exactly. I may have an idea of what's going on here," Rhyven said.

I looked at him, my gaze wide and questioning.

"Since I've been here on Earth, I've had some time to do my own research. I was always intrigued by the portal magic you possessed and wondered why no other fae in our realm has had it for so long," Rhyven continued. "I think you might have an ancient fairy magic that has been dormant in your body."

I frowned. That couldn't be it, could it? In the olden days, there were very powerful fae roaming Fairy, ones that had magic with full control over the natural world. They had the sort of magic that could defy even those of the court royals. A magic that combined all the elements of Fairy to give them a power unlike any other.

"But those were fairy tales," I said. "Things that parents told children before tucking them in at night. The ancient fae were nothing but a story. I thought they were a myth."

"Me too," Rhyven replied. "But seeing what you're doing here with the portals, the way the roses are changing color, and how your magic is manifesting ... Maybe they weren't stories after all."

My frown deepened. I buried my fingers into the earth, feeling it under my fingernails. Relief slowly crept into my body, as it did whenever I was close to the natural world. I breathed in the scent of the flowers surrounding me. In response, the roses stretched further, reaching for me like a child reaches for its mother.

"You see what I mean?" Rhyven said, pointing to one of the flower buds that had opened and bloomed right before our eyes. The bright orange hue shifted slightly, like it was about to change color again.

I scoffed. "I suppose we can't rule it out."

An idea slammed through me as I recalled the last few times I was able to open portals. My jaw slackened. My arms fell limp at my sides.

"What is it?" Rhyven asked.

"I just remembered the commonality between the time I left home and the time I opened the ice portal."

"What is it?" he asked again.

When I looked at him, he pressed his lips together into a tight line. "Oh ... You were afraid of me."

I nodded, wincing. "Sorry. In my defense, that was before I got to know you better."

"You're not afraid of me anymore?" Rhyven asked.

I laughed. "Let's go with that. Sure."

Before I could say another word, the prince stood up

and spread his arms wide to the side. Shadows burst from his body, encircling us in a typhoon of darkness. I screamed as they ripped at my hair and slapped at my skin.

"Rhyven! What are you doing? Stop!"

The prince sneered and threw his magic further. It slammed into me, crashing me to the ground until I couldn't breathe. My body was soaked with sweat, and my heart raced in my chest. I opened my mouth to scream, but the shadows shot into me. Suffocating me with their power. My eyes watered as I struggled to stand up, my own magic rushing to the surface. I threw my hands out to fight back but instead of fairy magic, sparkling light ignited from within me. I levitated off the ground, floating higher and higher until my feet dangled in the air. Terror struck through me as my own magic magnified. The thread of sparkle amplified and thrust forward. I gasped as a portal opened in the place where it hit a few feet away from Theo's sleeping form. My body shook as I looked at the cat, thinking, *That changeling could sleep through anything.*

A second later, Rhyven dropped his hold on me. His shadows rushed back into his body, disappearing and vanishing like they were never there. I dropped to the ground, sucking in sharp, painful breaths.

The prince was on me in seconds, helping me up.

"I'm so sorry," he whispered. "I thought it might help if I scared you."

We peeled our gazes off each other and looked at the portal. Beyond, flurries of snow danced before us, and the coldness emanating from the portal made my bones tremble.

"It definitely worked this time," I told the prince. "Good thinking. What now?"

Rhyven took my hand and brought it to his lips, kissing it lightly. The touch made shivers trip down my spine, and I pressed my legs together, trying to stay upright.

"I'll tell you what I find," Rhyven said, pushing away from me.

Before I could stop him, he zipped into the portal, leaping into it like a madman and leaving me behind. As he landed on the other side, the prince turned to wink at me.

"Rhyven!" I yelled.

My words were cut off because in that moment, the portal doorway slammed shut, closing the opening between me and the Prince of the Shadow Court. My pulse continued to thrum between my ears, a heavy headache forming behind my temples.

"I can't believe he did that," I whispered.

"Who did what?" Theo asked between yawns, finally getting up from his nap.

"Rhyven ..." I stumbled on my words. "He's gone."

As soon as the words left my mouth, the front doorbell rang out, making me jump. I leapt on the spot and glanced at the cat. My brows rose as I spun to look at Mistbrook Manor. Colorful lights bounced off the walls of the house and I heard the faint sounds of an ambulance siren approaching in the distance. I looked at the cat again, knowing full well what this meant.

Another body had arrived at the funeral home.

My heart sank into my boots. It really was true, what they said: There was no rest for the wicked. But there was even less rest for the dead.

About the Author

A.N. Sage is a bestselling, award-winning author of mystery and fantasy novels. She has spent most of her life waiting to meet a witch, vampire, or at least get haunted by a ghost. In between failed seances and many questionable outfit choices, she has developed a keen eye for the extra-ordinary.

A.N. spends her free time reading and binge-watching television shows in her pajamas. Currently, she resides in Toronto, Canada with her husband who is not a creature of the night and their daughter who just might be.

A.N. Sage is a Scorpio and a massive advocate of leggings for pants.

For more books and updates:

www.ansage.ca

Connect on social media:

Facebook Group:

facebook.com/groups/945090619339423/
Instagram:
instagram.com/a.n.sage/
YouTube:
youtube.com/c/ANSageWrites

www.ingramcontent.com/pod-product-compliance
Lightning Source LLC
Chambersburg PA
CBHW050310110726
47899CB00007B/2177